Trouble in Toadpool

Also by Anne Fine

Published by Corgi Books:

The Book Of The Banshee • The Granny Project • On The Summerhouse Steps
The Road Of Bones • Round Behind The Ice House • The Devil Walks
The Stone Menagerie • Up On Cloud Nine

Published by Corgi Yearling Books:

Bad Dreams • Charm School • Frozen Billy
The More The Merrier • Eating Things On Sticks

A Shame To Miss . . .

Three Collections Of Poetry
Perfect Poems For Young Readers • Ideal Poems For Middle Readers
Irresistible Poetry For Young Adults

Other books by Anne Fine

For junior readers:

The Angel Of Nitshill Road • Anneli The Art-Hater
Bill's New Frock • The Chicken Gave It To Me
The Country Pancake • Crummy Mummy And Me
Genie, Genie, Genie • How To Write Really Badly
Ivan The Terrible • The Killer Cat's Birthday Bash
Loudmouth Louis • A Pack Of Liars
Stories Of Jamie And Angus

For young people:

Flour Babies • Goggle-Eyes • Madame Doubtfire • Step By Wicked Step
The Tulip Touch • Very Different • Blood Family

For adult readers:

All Bones And Lies • Fly In The Ointment • The Killjoy
Raking The Ashes • Taking The Devil's Advice
Telling Liddy • Our Precious Lulu • In Cold Domain

www.annefine.co.uk

anne fine

Trouble in Toadpool

Illustrated by Kate Aldous

CORGI YEARLING

TROUBLE IN TOADPOOL
A CORGI YEARLING BOOK 978 0 440 86962 7

First published in Great Britain by Doubleday,
an imprint of Random House Children's Publishers UK
A Random House Group Company

Hardback edition published 2012
This edition published 2013

1 3 5 7 9 10 8 6 4 2

Set in Palatino

RANDOM HOUSE CHILDREN'S PUBLISHERS UK
61–63 Uxbridge Road, London W5 5SA

www.**randomhousechildrens**.co.uk
www.**totallyrandombooks**.co.uk
www.**randomhouse**.co.uk

Addresses for companies within The Random House Group Limited can be found at:
www.randomhouse.co.uk/offices.htm

THE RANDOM HOUSE GROUP Limited Reg. No. 954009

A CIP catalogue record for this book is available from the British Library.

Printed and bound in Great Britain by CPI Group (UK) Ltd, Croydon CR0 4YY

ACT ONE

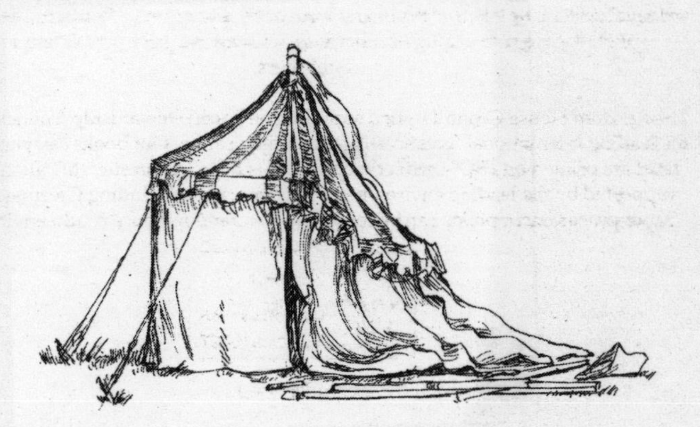

BINGO! MY HOMEWORK DONE!

So there I was, sitting quietly at the kitchen table, finishing my toast and getting on with my weekend homework. Our class was doing captions. We had to choose a photo of each member of our family and stick it in our workbook, then write a caption underneath.

'And do try to find a photo that gets the spirit of the person,' Mrs Bunford told us. 'Because the word caption comes from the Latin word "capere" which means to take or seize.'

I'd already done most of the family. I'd got Dad sitting against the garden shed, out of sight of the house. He was having a quick snooze and the caption I'd written was, 'James Mountfield doing his usual share of the chores.'

I'd stuck in a photo of Mum ticking somebody off. (I don't know who it was. It could have been any of us. Mum spends her whole life ticking people off.) I'd captioned it, 'My mum, telling someone what they ought to have done even before they've had time to explain what they did do.'

I'd found a photo of my Uncle Tristram on Christmas morning, passing the time by armpit squelching the tune of *The Teddy Bears' Picnic*. I'd called it, 'A pleasant musical interlude.'

My photo of Great-Granny was one Dad took while she was stomping down the Ballspond canal path, hissing at blackbirds and spitting at rabbits. The caption read, 'A nice day out in the country.'

There was a photo of the back of Harry's head. 'My handsome brother's best side,' I'd written.

Then I picked out a photo of my cousin Titania. It wasn't a hard choice. When I went through the nineteen billion photographs that my Aunt Susan has sent us, I found only one that wasn't of Titania prancing around a stage dressed as a milkmaid or fairy or princess. My cousin's almost my age. So rather than embarrass my whole family in front of Mrs Bunford, I chose that one. (Titania was in a tutu.)

'Great Big Fancy Show-Off,' I'd written.

It took an age to find a photo of Titania's dad. But finally I spotted one of him scrambling out of his car. I couldn't think of a caption – except for something I'd heard Mum mutter under her breath that seemed a bit too rude to write in ink in my workbook. Or, 'Utter menace on the road!' which Dad says often. So I left Uncle Digby for a bit, while I stuck in the very last photo I was going to do.

Aunt Susan, rounding everyone up for one of her ghastly nature walks.

I stared at it for a little while and then I said to Mum, 'What would you call the cruellest, bossiest woman in the world, forever herding people places they don't want to go?'

'Obergruppenführerin?' suggested Mum.

I snatched my pen up. 'Can you spell that, please?'

Off she went, patiently enough. 'O – b – e – r – g – r —'

Dad ambled into the kitchen halfway through. 'What are you spelling out for Ralph?'

'Obergruppenführerin,' said Mum.

'It's English homework,' I explained.

He grinned and asked Mum, 'Why? Has he been asked to write the perfect job description for your sister Susan?'

Then he leaned over my shoulder to peer at my workbook. Spotting the photo of Uncle Digby getting safely out of his car, he pointed. 'See that? A photo of one of life's great mysteries: The World's Worst Driver getting out of a car alive.'

Mrs Bunford said to try to keep our captions 'pithy'. So all I wrote was 'Uncle Digby, cheating Death.'

Bingo! My homework done! Now for a whole free day!

NO VISITORS, NO RELATIONS, NO PLANS AT ALL

I wasn't the only one who was delighted to have no plans for the day. Mum was already crowing. 'Bliss! A lovely, quiet, nothing-to-do and nothing-on-the-calendar Sunday.' She turned to Dad. 'How long has it been?'

'*Weeks,*' he said. 'First Uncle Tristram broke his leg. The weekend after that, the guttering fell down. Then there was all that business of trying to persuade Great-Granny not to appeal after her court case. Then that pipe burst. Then—'

'Stop!' ordered Mum. 'It's all behind us now. All we have facing us is a nice quiet day – the most relaxing for weeks.' She switched on the kettle. 'Who's for a cup of tea?'

Harry and I raised our hands. Dad panted like a dog to show her he was keen as well, and then we all sat quietly, in contemplation of the perfect day. No visitors. No relations. No plans at all. Homework all done. Nothing to organize.

'I know,' said Dad. 'To celebrate, I'll tell you all a joke.'

We turned to face him.

'There are three robbers,' he began. 'They're on the run from their last burglary, and gradually they hear the police-car sirens getting closer behind them.'

He waited. Usually, at this point, one of the three of us pipes up to say, 'Heard it already.' But this time nobody spoke.

'Right,' he said,

somewhat unnerved. 'So the robbers abandon their getaway car and run off with their swag across a field. On the far side they see a barn and rush inside to look for somewhere to hide. The only things that they can see are three dirty old sacks. So each of them snatches one up and jumps inside it.'

Still no one was claiming to remember the joke he was telling us, so he kept on. 'But the police have followed the robbers across the field into the barn. They storm in and look around. All they can see is three dirty old sacks. They're still suspicious, so they kick the first sack really hard, and the robber inside thinks quickly and then pretends he's a chicken.'

Harry did his excellent imitation of a hen. 'Cluck, *cluck*! Cluck, cluck, *cluck*!'

'Exactly so,' said Dad. 'So the police officers are fooled. Then, just in case – in order to be thorough – they kick the next sack really hard. But the robber who's hiding inside that one is just as quick-thinking as the first, and, taking a cue from his mate, he hastily pretends he's a pig.'

I'm better than Harry at making pig noises. 'Oink, *oink*! Oink, oink, oink, *oink*!'

'Yes, just like that,' Dad said.

The phone began to ring.

Ignoring it, Dad carried on. 'So finally the police move on to the third sack.'

The phone kept ringing. 'Get that, would you, Jamie?' prompted Mum. 'I'm in the middle of pouring tea.'

Dad slid off his stool and went towards the phone, saying, 'And just to make absolutely sure, one of the police officers kicks the third sack very hard indeed and—'

Copping a look from Mum, he picked the phone off its cradle. 'Hello? James Mountfield speaking. Who is this?'

We all watched as the blood drained from his face.

YES, SUSAN . . . YES, SUSAN . . .
YES, SUSAN . . .

That only happens when Aunt Susan calls. Usually Mum just takes over. But since she hadn't had her tea she wasn't up for it, so she shook her head to signal that he should take the call.

Still looking ashen, Dad turned his attention back to the barrage pouring into his left ear.

We all sat listening.

'Yes, Susan. Yes . . . Really? Dear me! Yes, I can see that's going to be a horrid nuisance for them . . . Yes, they must be in a pickle. But these things happen, and there's nothing to be done except to—'

We watched him freeze. 'I'm sorry, Susan. What was that you said?' He shot us all a desperate look. '*Us?* Oh, no! Oh, no! I'm sorry, Susan, but we all have plans fixed for today.'

There was a horrid pause.

'*What* plans?' Dad gazed around with a hunted look. 'Well, Ralph has arranged to go swimming.'

It was the first I'd heard of it.

'And Harry's off to see a film with friends.'

Harry looked startled but pleased.

'Tansy?' Dad looked at Mum who flapped her hands at him and mouthed quite clearly, 'Don't you dare!' So, 'Oh, no,' he answered down the phone. 'Tansy can't come. No chance. She's got the most frightful cold. In fact, she's been in bed all week. Why, the poor lamb can scarcely stand. She couldn't possibly come all the way down to Toadpool today.'

There was more of a barrage down the

phone, and then we heard Dad's strangled, '*Me*? Lord, no! I simply can't. You see, I—'

Invention failed him.

'Well, I can't. I'm sorry, Susan. I just *can't*.'

Another great bombardment down the phone. More looks of horror from my dad. Then the retreat. 'Well, we'd be frightfully late . . . I know it only takes an hour and a half to drive down there. It's just that we have things to do before— Yes, Susan, I do understand that it's important, and there's no one else, but— Yes, Susan . . . Yes, Susan . . . Yes, Susan . . . Yes, we'll do that. Yes, right now, Susan . . . Yes, we're already getting in the car. Yes, we'll be there in no time at all . . . No, we won't let you down . . . Yes, we'll be there.'

He put the phone down.

Mum carefully replaced her mug of tea on the kitchen counter. 'Who is this "we"?' she asked him icily. 'Who is this "we" who is expected somewhere in no time at all?'

Dad's hunted look got worse. Then he changed tack and pointed a finger at Mum accusingly. 'This is *your* fault.

You know perfectly well that I can't cope with your sister. You should have known to take the call. So it's your fault, not mine.'

'What is her fault, not yours?' asked Harry. 'And where are we suddenly supposed to be going?'

Mum turned her back on Dad. 'I am not going anywhere,' she said. 'It seems I have the most frightful cold and have been in bed all week. Indeed, it appears that I can barely stand. So where would I be going?'

'Me neither,' Harry said. 'Since it seems I'm off to see a film.'

I wasn't going to be left out. 'Nor me,' I said. 'I can't come either since you told me that I'm going swimming.'

'Oh, stop it, all of you!' wailed Dad. 'You can't bail out on me like this. She's not *my* sister. Or *my* aunt.' He dropped his head in his hands. 'Oh, why can't we ever have a blissful, lovely, quiet, nothing-to-do and nothing-on-the-calendar Sunday? Is this some Mountfield family *curse*?'

NOW, LOOK HERE, SUSAN . . .

I thought the idea of a curse was rather good. Something to boast about in school. But Mum had other ideas.

'No!' she said. 'I will not have this. I am phoning back.'

She must have seen our looks of utter horror.

'Why not?' she persisted. 'Susan is only a person, after all. She's not the Witch of Endor or a contract killer.'

'She might be,' Dad tried to warn. But Mum was already punching in her sister's number, so we all watched, open-mouthed, as she said firmly, 'Susan? I need to talk to you ab—'

She didn't get too far.

'No, Susan. We're not in the car yet. And— No, Susan, because— No, Susan. I'm afraid— Now, look here, Susan . . .'

She reached out for her cup of tea, but it was far too late. Already her tone was weakening. 'Yes, I remember that. And you were very helpful . . . Yes, Susan, I do recall that, and you're right. Without your help, we'd never have— Yes, Susan. That was very helpful indeed of you and Digby . . .'

Gradually Mum's spine was sliding down the front of the kitchen cabinets till she was sitting on the floor, her legs outstretched. 'Yes, Susan . . . Yes, I see . . . Yes, Susan. Yes . . .'

And she switched off the phone.

'Well done!' Dad said sarcastically. 'Excellent going, Tansy! The fort well held!'

Mum tried to defend herself. 'She didn't leave me with a leg to stand on.'

Dad pointed to her, sprawling on the floor. 'So we all see.'

Mum scrambled to her feet. 'It wasn't my fault. First she went on about that time she took us all in after Harry filled the house with fleas.'

My brother rolled his eyes. He's always getting stick about those fleas, but it was Mum's fault. She's always ticking people off for their poor manners. All Harry did was help some poor old tramp into his coat. He wasn't to know the horrors that would follow.

'That was the longest week,' sighed Dad. 'And even after we got back, the house *stank* of insecticide.'

'Then she pitched in about lending you all that money in a hurry last summer.'

'That wasn't *all* my fault,' said Dad. 'Everyone has dreams so vivid that they think they're real. I truly did believe I'd bought those flight tickets and put them safely in the holiday wallet. You should have double-checked.'

Mum didn't bother arguing about all that again. She only said, 'Then she reminded me that it was she and Digby who found and paid for that amazing barrister who overturned your grandmother's conviction on appeal.'

Dad shook his head. 'I truly don't know how the woman did it. Why, everyone in the home was watching when Natasha smashed the vase down on that poor fellow's head. How any court in the land could have—'

Mum interrupted him. 'And so we're going down to help.'

'With what?' asked Harry.

'The Great Toadpool Show.'

TAKE OFF THOSE STUPID RABBIT SLIPPERS

'What's the Great Toadpool Show?'

Mum looked at Harry as if he only had one teaspoonful of brain, and that was in the freezer.

'I know!' I said. 'I bet it's a show they have in Great Toadpool.'

'Oh, give the boy a coconut!' scoffed Dad.

Already, you will notice, all of us were getting ratty. But that's Aunt Susan for you. Everywhere she goes, hearts sink and spirits plummet. Her charity carol singing evenings are grim. Her village history walks are worse. And Dad says if she drags us down to watch Titania prancing around the Toadpool maypole one more time, he's going to strangle both of them with their own ribbons.

'It isn't just a *show,*' Mum told us. 'It's a competition of children's choirs. But last year's judges complained they hadn't enough time to do the judging properly. So this year there were to be some acts on stage to fill the time before the winners are announced.'

She turned to Dad. 'She said she told you all this.'

'She did,' said Dad. 'She said the Toadpool Ladies' Charity Guild had booked some entertainers, but for the wrong date. So when they rang this morning in a panic, they found that two were off on holiday, one's at a wedding, one is visiting his mother, and one's not answering the phone.'

'Smarter than you, then,' said Mum.

Dad pointedly ignored the jibe. 'So,' he said. 'Trouble in Toadpool. The Ladies' Charity Guild are in a real pickle.'

'Yes,' Mum said bitterly. 'Until my sister claimed that she could save the day.'

We all know why. Aunt Susan's desperate to join the Toadpool Ladies' Charity Guild, but there are only ever twelve of them, and they're full up. They share Aunt Susan's passion for bossing everyone about; and since they make tons of money for starving orphans and homeless ducks and crumbling hospitals and stuff, everyone has to let them.

Just then, Harry handed his phone to Dad. 'Here, look at this.'

Mum and I leaned across to see as well. It was a web page. Dad scrolled down and we all read it.

Come along to
the Annual Great Toadpool Choir Competition
2-4 p.m. on Sunday September 23rd
Plus!! Added Show & Outdoor Attractions!!
Fortune Teller
Acrobats
Poetry Recitation
Lucky Dip
Stilt-walker
Unicycle Display
Raffle
Pixie Song
and
A Mystery Celebrity Guest

Now Mum looked baffled. 'I don't get this at all. If Susan's to look halfway organized enough to join the Guild, she'll need the acts that have been advertised.' She ticked them off on her fingers. 'She'll need a fortune teller, acrobats, a unicycle rider and someone to walk about on stilts.' She looked around at all of us. 'And none of us can ride a unicycle or walk about on stilts, or do fancy acrobatics.'

'I can hang upside down on a trapeze,' I said, 'and thread my legs through.'

While they were staring at me in contempt, honesty triumphed. 'Well,' I admitted, 'sometimes I can thread my legs through, and sometimes they get stuck.'

Harry was not to be outdone. 'I can't do proper stilts,' he said, 'but I can walk around on Albert's upside-down plastic flowerpot things on strings.'

'Those upside-down plastic flowerpot things on strings are just for *toddlers*,' I scoffed. 'That's why Albert was given them. Because he's only three.'

'None the less,' Harry said, 'I've been in next door's garden quite a lot this summer, and now I am quite good at walking around on them.'

We looked at Mum and Dad, to see if they had anything to offer.

'I'm still quite nifty on a normal bike,' admitted Dad. 'Wheelies and such. How hard can unicycles be?'

'Quite hard,' said Mum. 'That is why people pay to see those who can ride them.'

'If we set off now,' Dad said, 'I would have time to practise when we got there. And find out who's the Mystery Celebrity Guest.'

'No mystery who'll be singing the Pixie Song,' I said, because Aunt Susan has only organized us into sitting and listening to Titania warble it a hundred times.

'Pity she isn't doing her Fairy Tumbling Act,' said Harry, and he and I fell to sniggering, remembering last time we saw Titania on stage. She toppled over doing one of her fancy handstands and fell on the boards. A lump of freshly-chewed gum stuck to her knicker frills, and when she scrambled to her feet we saw a flash of bottom.

'I expect Titania's doing the Poetry Recitation as well,' sighed Mum.

Harry launched into one of his brilliant imitations of our cousin. '"*Four baby thwallows thang a happy thong.*"'

I chimed in with the second line. '"*The thun thyon down the whole day long.*"'

'Knock that off, both of you,' warned Mum. Bowing to fate, she poured the dregs of her tea away down the plug hole. 'All right,' she sighed. 'Action stations.'

'I'll go next door and get those flowerpot things off Albert,' Harry said.

Mum rolled her eyes, muttering, 'I can't believe my sister expects this family to fill in for real professional entertainers.'

'I'll get the flowerpots anyway,' said Harry. 'Just in case.'

Mum sighed. 'Well, you know Albert. So don't forget to wheedle properly or you'll get bitten.' She turned to me. 'Ralph, take off those stupid rabbit slippers and put on sensible shoes.' An anxious look spread over her face. She turned to Dad and asked him fearfully, 'James, you do think Susan will come to her senses, don't you? She'll realize that we can't actually perform on stage?'

'Of course she will!' Dad assured her. 'You know your sister. She could organize an Arctic expedition before lunch, and still have time to check her bank statement. Why, by the time we arrive, she will have rounded up whole troupes of acrobats and stilt-walkers and such, and all she'll want from us is moral support for a long day.'

'I hope you're right,' said Mum. (She didn't sound too sure.) 'In any case, we must show willing. I'll nip upstairs to fetch one or two things that might be useful. James, you go out and open the garage doors. And I want everyone sitting in the car ready to go in—' She glanced at the kitchen clock. 'Four minutes exactly.'

And that was the last that any of us saw of our blissful, lovely, quiet, nothing-to-do and nothing-on-the-calendar Sunday.

GREAT-GRANNY'S PRIVATE PORTAL TO HELL

Mum bagged the driver's seat, then leaned across with some old rag that looked a bit like a floor cloth. 'Could you shift back, James, so I can shove this in the glove pocket?'

Dad forced himself to lean a little further back. When Mum is at the wheel, he hunches forward, scouring the road ahead like someone taking a reckless teenage tearaway out for her first lesson. I let Dad concentrate on worrying until we reached a straight and empty patch of road, and then asked hopefully, 'Will Uncle Tristram be there as well?'

Dad didn't answer.

Harry repeated my question. Dad turned to tick us off. 'I'll thank you two not to distract your mother while she's concentrating on traffic.'

'She is a better driver than you,' I pointed out. 'You've had two prangs in the last year, and Mum has never hit anything.'

Into the frosty silence that greeted this remark, I asked the question a third time. 'Did Aunt Susan say anything about Uncle Tristram coming?'

'No,' Dad said, adding somewhat gloomily, 'But I expect he will.'

'I'm not so sure,' said Mum. 'He's not allowed to drive with that cast on his leg.'

'Digby will have been sent to collect him. That probably explains why we're the ones who have to give a lift to Great-Granny.'

Mum braked so hard the seat belt saved my life. 'Are we supposed to be picking up your grandmother?'

Dad squirmed in his seat. 'Yes, Susan did mention it.'

'And you *agreed*?'

Dad offered vaguely, 'I don't remember actually *arguing*.'

I thought I'd try to be helpful. 'That is because you didn't argue,' I reminded him. 'Once she got going, the only words you managed to get out were, "Yes, Susan", "Yes, we'll do that" and "Yes. Right now".'

'Well, thanks a bunch, James!' said Mum. 'You know that, once the boys' great-granny gets in, each car journey we make turns into a perfect nightmare.'

Dad tried to defend himself. 'Well, it was all a bit of a rush – what with Ralph not being able to find his shoes, and you hurling ancient leotards around the bedroom, and Harry coming back dripping with blood from borrowing Albert's flowerpots.'

'That bite still hurts,' complained Harry.

'It's your own fault,' I told him. 'You know that Albert can't be rushed into sharing his toys. Mum made a point of telling you not to skimp on the wheedling.'

'There wasn't *time* to wheedle properly,' Harry pointed out. 'If you remember, Mum gave us exactly four minutes to gather everything and get in the car.'

'I don't know why we had to hurry,' I

mentioned to the air around us, 'since we're just sitting here at the side of the road, going exactly nowhere.'

Mum was still glaring at Dad. 'You told my sister we would bring Great-Granny down with us?'

'Susan insisted,' Dad explained. 'Perhaps she thinks Natasha can tell fortunes.'

'I'm sure she can,' said Mum, 'along with casting the evil eye, and opening her Private Portal to Hell.' She slid the car back into gear and then, still sounding sour, she picked on Harry and me. 'Well, at the very least,' she said, 'you boys can do us all a favour and get your tiresome squabbling about who does or doesn't want to sit beside Great-Granny's handbag over and done with before she even gets in.'

WOULD YOU LIKE A SWEETIE, LITTLE BOY?

I *love* Great-Granny's care home. You go into Appleby Grange, and you come out with pockets full of sweets. Whole pockets full! There's this old lady who sits in the lobby, pouncing on you each time you pass. 'Would you like a sweetie, little boy?' I don't know what she was before she was ancient. Maybe a sweet-shop owner. Or a dentist with not enough patients. Maybe even a serial poisoner. All I know is that now she sits in her wheelchair all day long handing out boiled sweets, and she is so far gone she doesn't realize it's the same boy – me – who's walking in and out of the glass doors and past her, over and over.

'Do have a sweetie, little boy.'

'Little boy, do you fancy a sweet?'

'Can I offer you a sweetie, young man?'

While I was gratefully accepting my thirtieth striped mint, a carer who'd been eyeing me for quite a while drifted a little nearer. I thought I'd get a ticking off and have to hand back my ill-gotten gains. But no.

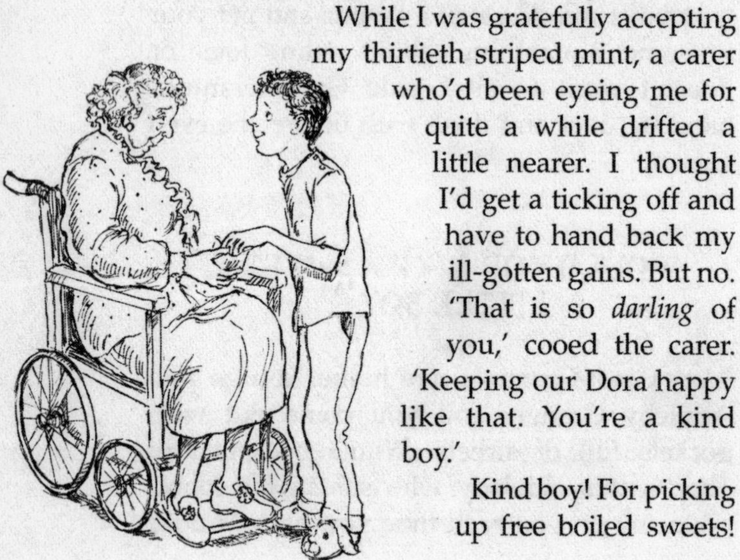

'That is so *darling* of you,' cooed the carer. 'Keeping our Dora happy like that. You're a kind boy.'

Kind boy! For picking up free boiled sweets!

I think I'd *live* in an old people's home if I could wangle it. All that loud telly blaring out all day, with no one ever bellowing at you to turn it down. Mucking about in the corridors in battery-powered chairs and scooters on wheels that (if you have the strength to press the knobs) can go quite fast. Not feeling weird because you couldn't find your sensible shoes and are still wearing furry rabbit slippers. Boxes of chocolates lying open on every chair and table, and no one having the faintest memory of who it was who bought them or whose they are.

Bliss! Utter bliss!

'Would you like a sweetie, little boy?'

I saw the others spilling out of the lift, herding Great-Granny in front of them. As soon as Mum was close enough to overhear, I told Dora virtuously, 'No. Thank you, but I'd better not. I'm not allowed to eat sweets in case I get holes in my teeth.'

DIGBY

Mum favoured me with a proud smile and I fell in behind the little procession. Catching me unawares as we went down the steps, Harry elbowed me onto Great-Granny's handbag side. (We hate that handbag. We reckon it is full of rocks because, if you sit next to it, you get huge bruises that don't fade for weeks.)

Just as Harry grinned in triumph, Great-Granny shifted the horrid thing from one arm to the other. Instantly, Harry tried to elbow himself back to the safe side, but I was more alert now, and I wouldn't let him.

Mum has eyes in the back of her head. 'You two stop that right now!'

We carried on, scuffling more quietly. But Harry's stronger, so I changed my plan. I thought I'd wait until Great-Granny was settled in the middle of the car's back seat, then leap in on whichever side she hadn't stowed the handbag.

Great-Granny jammed the bag of rocks down on her left-hand side. I took a dive to the right, saying, 'Let me fasten you in!' As I leaned over, I distinctly heard Great-Granny growl. But I was brave and pulled her seat belt across. Then I slid in beside her.

Scowling, Harry got in on the other side, and I leaned forward so I could smirk at him across Great-Granny.

Great-Granny curled her lip and snarled at me, 'Still acting the bucket-head, I see.'

'I don't know what you mean,' I told her frostily.

'Head full of doors, and all of them banging in the wind.'

'I think she's calling you stupid,' Harry helpfully explained.

I cracked. 'Shut up, you goblin!'

'You too, cockroach!'

'Must I sit next to these two lunatics?' Great-Granny asked.

'It won't be long,' Dad lied. 'We'll be at Upper Toadpool in two shakes of a lamb's tail.'

'That's still too long to sit beside these idiot articles,' Great-Granny sniffed, and lifted her handbag to her chest to root in it for a while. Either the rock that she was looking for was not inside or she forgot which of them she wanted, because after a minute or two of furtive clanking she snapped the clasp shut, lifted the handbag in the air –

Then jammed it down on my side.

I spent the next ten minutes staring out of the window so Harry wouldn't get the satisfaction of seeing me seeing him smirk. It wasn't too dull because my dad keeps up a running commentary about the other drivers on the road. 'Fool!' 'Dimwit!' 'Buy yourself some specs, mate!' and, 'That's right! Don't wear your indicators out. Always best not to use them.'

Finally I risked turning back, only to see that Harry was absorbed in *Box of Frogs* on his phone. Since they were already hopping in the cereal bowl, on Level 3, he must have been at it the whole time I had been pretending to admire the scenery.

Dad started off again. 'Where do these bean-brains *come* from? Look at this guy in front! He can't decide which way to go. He indicates one way, then turns the other. Half the time he's crawling along at fifteen miles an hour, then, just as you get a bit of straight road where you might get a chance to overtake, the fool speeds up.'

Harry and I both looked, then turned to grin at one another across Great-Granny.

'I don't know where they *find* these people,' Dad went on. 'There must be an Idiot Driver Factory somewhere, churning them out.' He clutched his head. 'Oh, no! He's turning down the Toadpool road! That means that we'll be stuck behind him the whole of the rest of the way now.'

'That'll be fine,' said Mum, 'so long as you stop harping on about him.'

'After all,' Harry said sweetly, 'it isn't nice – what with him being family.'

'Family?' Dad peered through the windscreen. But since the rear-view mirror in the car ahead was sharply angled to the floor, he couldn't catch even a glimpse of the driver's face.

'Look at the number plate,' I said.

D1G 6Y.

'You two knew all along!' said Dad. 'You let me just go on and on, and all the time you—'

Without warning, Uncle Digby braked to let a leaf blow over the road in front of him. Mum braked as hard, to avoid ramming Digby's posh new number plate. We all slammed into our seat belts and Great-Granny's handbag hurtled forward, catching Dad on the ear.

'Yee-ouch! That *hurt*!'

'Oh, do be quiet,' Mum said testily, 'or I shall have to move Natasha into the front and ask you to sit with the boys.'

The back of Dad's neck went pink, but

whether it was from embarrassment or fury I couldn't tell.

'Who is that in the passenger seat?' I asked.

But just then Uncle Digby picked up speed to go round all the hairpin bends and over the blind humps that lead to Upper and Lower Toadpool. Mum kept her distance in case more leaves blew anywhere, so it was not until we pulled up outside Aunt Susan's house that we saw who'd been in the car, sitting beside Digby.

'Yeah! Uncle Tristram!'

ACT TWO

FORTUNE
TELLING

NOT A CELEBRITY. OR A MYSTERY. OR EVEN MUCH OF A GUEST

I ran towards Uncle Tristram, who held out his hands to fend me off. 'Mind my leg! Don't come too near! The slightest movement jars it horribly!'

'For heaven's sake!' said Mum. 'You've had that cast on for *weeks* and *weeks*! Your leg must be mended by now.'

I thought that wasn't very sisterly, and so I said, more sympathetically, 'You do look pale.'

'That's not the leg,' said Uncle Tristram. 'That is Digby's driving. I've no idea which testing station gave the man a licence, but it should be closed down. He indicates one way then turns the other. All he can see in the mirror is his own feet. Half the time he's crawling along; then, just as the poor soul in the car behind gets a sniff of straight road, the idiot speeds up.' He spread his hands despairingly. 'As for the way he took those hairpin bends and those blind humps, don't even start me off! If I'd had the slightest idea what horrors lay in store, I'd have told Susan when she rang that I'd a frightful cold.'

'Take it from me, that didn't work,' said Mum.

'Then I'd have said that I was going to the cinema.'

Now it was Harry's turn. 'That didn't work either.'

Uncle Tristram swivelled to face me. 'Off swimming?'

Sadly, I shook my head.

'Oh, well,' he said. 'At least I know I'm not here just because I was too daft to make a quick excuse.'

'I don't see why she wants you anyway,' said Mum. 'You can't do much that's useful with that cast on your leg.'

'He could sell raffle tickets,' I suggested.

'Sell raffle tickets?' Uncle Tristram looked a bit put out. 'Why should your Aunt Susan need *me* to sell raffle tickets? Any fool can do that! No, I'm sure that she's got me down for something far more important.'

'Like what?' demanded Mum. 'With that thing on your leg you can't do acrobatics or walk around on stilts or ride a unicycle.'

'Perhaps not. But I have been studying the list of attractions, and I suspect I'm here to fill in for the Mystery Celebrity Guest.'

All of us stared.

'But you're not a Celebrity,' I finally offered.

'Or even much of a Mystery,' Dad said, 'once one has accepted that you have a psychopathic bent.'

Mum put the last boot in. 'And being family, roped in like this at the last minute, you couldn't really argue that you're much of a Guest.'

'None the less,' Uncle Tristram told us loftily, 'I expect that is what I'm going to be.'

Mum argued stubbornly, 'I don't see how.' But she had clearly piqued his pride because he swivelled on his cast and peg-legged off.

'Well, for the moment,' we heard floating back, 'that may have to remain a very small part of the Mystery.'

WATCH YOUR FAT LIP!

We stood and watched as Uncle Tristram hobbled out of sight.

'Not like your brother to get in a snit,' Dad said to Mum.

She shrugged. 'I expect he's practising.'

'What? Being a celebrity? Well, it's not going to work. No more than Harry walking around on flowerpots would make up for someone on stilts, or Ralph doing roly-polies in one of your old leotards would be an acrobatic performance.'

I tell you, I was *horrified*. I turned to Mum. 'That droopy rag you shoved in the glove compartment! Is that a *leotard*? And even if it is, I certainly hope you weren't expecting *me* to wear it!'

'You said that you could do trapeze tricks,' Mum defended herself.

'In trousers!' I yelled at her. 'Maybe in shorts, if it was really hot. Not in a *leotard*. And only one trick anyway. And even that only *sometimes*.'

'Come now,' teased Dad. 'Remember the famous saying: The show must go on.'

'No!' I said. 'Absolutely not!' And I ran back to fetch the leotard so I could stretch it out in front of Mum to show her how impossible it would have been for me to wear it. In public. Doing roly-polies. Or even on a trapeze. As I reached into the car, I heard an evil hiss and swung round to see Great-Granny, still strapped in the back, looking as wild as a bulldog that has just realized that it's chewing a wasp.

She snarled, 'Did you intend to leave me here all day?'

I told her for the millionth time, 'Look, all you have to do is press this little — *Ouch!*'

She'd slapped out. 'Put that hand near me again and I will rip it off and chew it in front of you.'

I shrank back, pointing. 'Press that red bit there.'

Still glowering horribly, she pressed the seat belt catch.

'See?' I said. 'It's really easy.'

'Watch your fat lip!' she snarled, and started shifting her great bottom towards the far side door. Once I was sure that I was safely out of range, I leaned in once again to pull out the leotard. It was about a thousand sizes too big. Even if it did not fall off me straight away, its bottom would sag round my knees.

On my way back I bumped into Aunt Susan, who was hurrying in through the side gate that leads to the village hall. Her eyes fell on my furry rabbit slippers. I think she was about to say something. But maybe a touch of evil had seeped out through Great-Granny's Private Portal into me, because I suddenly let rip with a black killer stare.

And my Aunt Susan backed right off.

ONE OR TWO LITTLE SCUFFLES . . .

Instead, Aunt Susan turned to greet the rest of the family. 'Tansy!' She peered at Mum more closely. 'How very strange! James said that you were flat out with the most appalling cold, but you look fine to me. Tip top!'

Mum blushed. 'Oh, well. You know. Once one is on the mend . . .'

Luckily, her sister didn't take the time to listen. 'Oh, don't I know it!' she cried, and swung round to face the rest of us. 'James! Harry! Ralph! Thank heavens you were all free!'

Harry said virtuously, 'I wasn't really. I was off to see a film with friends.'

Dad shot my brother a warning look. But since it was Dad's own bare-faced lie that Harry was recycling, he didn't have the nerve to tell him off. That made me brave enough to pitch in too. 'I wasn't either. I had arranged to go swimming.'

Aunt Susan said distractedly, 'Well, we must

all make sacrifices since I need everyone I can get.' Even as she was saying it, she threw a dubious glance towards Great-Granny, who had set off towards the flowerbeds, still looking in the mood to chew stones. Then, shrugging off her fears, Aunt Susan turned back.

'Now listen, everyone. We only have a couple of hours to get things sorted.' She pointed over her garden fence. 'We're putting all the usual stuff out there on the green around the hall.'

'The usual stuff?' said Dad.

She looked at him as if he was a halfwit. 'You know. The bran tub for the lucky dip. The raffle-ticket table. The fortune-telling tent. The jam stall. All that sort of thing.'

'Of course,' said Dad. 'All the usual stuff.'

Aunt Susan didn't catch the note of sarcasm. She just powered on. 'The choir competition itself will, of course, take place in the village hall. I calculate that the last choir will finish singing at approximately seven minutes past three.'

Dad rolled his eyes. This is the sort of thinking, he always says, that makes Aunt Susan better fitted to organize a moon probe than run a family.

'And everyone in the hall will have to be kept entertained until quarter to four. That's when the judges come out to declare the winner. And after that, we have one final combined song, and it's all over.'

'Thirty-three minutes, then,' said Mum. 'That's not too bad, is it? So who have you managed to round up at the last minute to save the day?'

Aunt Susan stared. 'Well, you and James, of course. And Tristram.' She waved a hand at me and Harry. 'And the boys.'

'Yes,' Mum agreed. 'We're all here to help out. But who have you found while we were driving down here who can do the actual entertainments?'

There was a rather long silence as Aunt Susan stared at Mum, clearly a bit baffled.

Mum turned on Dad and hissed, 'You said that you were absolutely sure—'

Already Harry had broken in. 'I'm going to be the stilt-walker,' he told Aunt Susan proudly. 'And Ralph here says that he can do trapeze tricks.'

'Not in a *leotard,*' I wailed.

Aunt Susan beamed. 'Trapeze tricks? Now that is excellent! And I know there's an old trapeze in the hall storage cupboard. I'll send Digby over straight away to root it out and hang it from a stage beam.'

'Fiasco in the making,' my father murmured.

Mum looked a little anxious too. 'Digby? Are you quite sure that Digby's the right person to—'

Aunt Susan swatted away my parents' worries. 'Nonsense! Digby's an excellent handyman. He is already putting up the fortune teller's tent.'

Dad muttered sourly, 'Really? In that case I don't think you'll need anyone sitting inside it to prophesy more havoc on the way.'

If my Aunt Susan heard this, she managed to ignore it. Mum interrupted fast. 'Where are the Ladies of the Toadpool Charity Guild?'

'They're busy setting out the chairs. And making sure they're labelled properly.' Aunt Susan dropped her voice. 'The Guild have had their troubles in the past, it seems, with this event.'

'Troubles?'

Aunt Susan waved a vague hand. 'Oh, you know. A bit of friendly rivalry between the choirs of various schools. A bit of cat-calling. Some paper flicking. One or two little scuffles.' She shrugged the small unpleasantness off. 'Best, say the Ladies, to keep everyone apart . . .'

'Susan,' said Mum. 'You hadn't thought that it might be better simply to make an announcement from the stage after the last choir finishes that there will be a longer interval than usual, and everyone might as well take the chance to go out for a breath of fresh air?'

The grim look on her sister's face hardened. 'Nonsense!' Aunt Susan said. 'I've told the Toadpool Ladies that I can offer thirty-three minutes of first-class indoor entertainment, and I will!'

TANSY, ARE YOU INSANE?

I think Mum might have kept on arguing, but right then we all heard a steady *scrunch-scrunch* noise, and turned to see my Uncle Tristram peg-legging back to us over the gravel. Usually he only has to catch a glimpse of his sister and he is sidling off the other way in case she rounds us up to sit and watch her precious Titania sing a new song, or dance a new dance, or recite some ghastly, sickly, home-made poem about a lost puppy or a poorly bird. But this time, treating the rest of us as if we were invisible, he hobbled up to grasp Aunt Susan's hands and squeeze them warmly. Slapping on a gracious I-know-I'm-famous-but-I-haven't-forgotten-that-at-heart-I'm-still-a-person-just-like-you smile, he told her loftily, 'Susan! I wouldn't have let you down for all the world!'

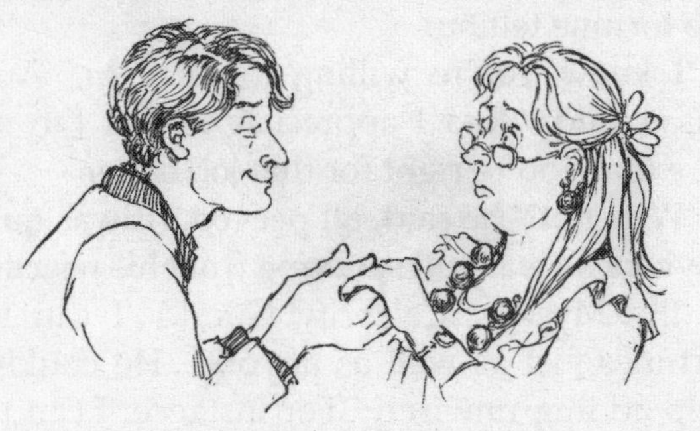

You could tell that Aunt Susan was startled. But instead of rolling her eyes (like Dad was doing) or sniggering (like Mum) she simply said to my uncle, 'Tristram, you're sweet. It's good of you to help me out like this. And, honestly, there's really not much to it.'

'No,' Uncle Tristram said with fetching modesty. 'I shall just try to be myself.'

Aunt Susan looked mystified. 'Be yourself? But why on earth shouldn't you?'

'He thinks he's going to be the Mystery Celebrity Guest,' Mum explained.

Aunt Susan stared at Tristram. 'But you're not a Celebrity. Or a Mystery. And, being my brother, I don't think you're really even what one might call a proper Guest.'

'Just what we told him,' chortled Mum.

Uncle Tristram gave up then, and started acting normally. 'All right. I don't mind. I'll do the fortune telling.'

'I know you're willing to pitch in,' Aunt Susan said. 'And I appreciate it. But I'm not sure that you're right for that job either.'

'Why not?' he said, all peeved. (It was quite obvious he was still smarting from his rejection as the Mystery Celebrity Guest.) 'I can tell fortunes just as well as anyone.' He couldn't help adding unwisely, 'For instance, I can tell you now that if Digby carries on driving half as badly as he did this morning, he won't keep his licence for much longer.'

Aunt Susan's eyes narrowed. 'Tristram, that sort of quite unnecessary unpleasantness simply confirms my suspicion that you would not undertake the role in the right charitable spirit.'

'In any case,' Harry informed him, 'Mum says Great-Granny is already booked to tell the fortunes.'

Aunt Susan looked startled. 'Natasha?'

'Because of her evil and mysterious powers,' Harry explained.

Aunt Susan was staring at Mum now. 'Tansy, are you *insane*? Invite Natasha to tell fortunes? Why, people would be running screaming from the tent, pulling their hair out!'

'Why did we have to bring her down here, then?' demanded Mum.

'To supervise the lucky dip, of course.' Aunt Susan shuddered. 'Last year it seems a swarm of horrid children bought tickets, then rooted in the bran tub for minutes on end, unwrapping all the gifts and feeling them all over to work out which were the expensive ones they'd seen on the posters. Then they pulled those out of the bran and left all the cheap ones behind.' She put on a determined look. 'Well, I'm not having that happen on my watch!'

Dragging other people's children off on boring walks to look at twigs and buds and stupid empty snail shells is one thing. Letting an elderly fiend loose to poke at them with her stick is quite another. There was a silence while we all imagined Great-Granny spitting fire at some poor toddler who meant well enough, but hadn't understood the simple rules of lucky dipping.

Mum tried another tack. 'Right, then. Why don't we just put only the cheaper gifts into the bran tub?'

'I thought of that,' Aunt Susan said (and you could tell that she'd been very tempted). 'But the Guild already fear that they might be at risk of being accused of selling tickets on false pretences – especially with their Mystery Celebrity Guest not showing up.'

'They think the Mystery Celebrity Guest is really that important?'

Aunt Susan stared at Mum. 'That is the only reason most people have bought tickets at all! You won't believe how many have been wriggling out of it, saying they heard the choirs last year. And the year before. And the year before that.'

'And probably heard Titania sing her pixie song a million times,' I muttered.

'And had an earful of her tragic poetry recitations,' sighed Uncle Tristram.

'She could put on her brand new fairy tumbling act,' said Harry, catching my eye, 'complete with chewing gum pratfall and display of knickers.'

Together we snickered quietly.

If Aunt Susan even heard, she definitely

ignored us. 'But then a whisper ran around that the Mystery Celebrity Guest was going to be Bruce Forsyth. We sold eight tickets. Eight! Even before lunch! Then someone else said that they'd heard that wasn't true, and just a story put about to keep the paparazzi off the scent because it was really going to be Robbie Williams. Then we sold sixty more tickets. And yesterday a rumour flew about that it might be Madonna and every last ticket's gone. So, yes! The Mystery Celebrity Guest is really, really important.'

Dad asked the question in all our minds. 'So, tell us, who was it going to be?'

Aunt Susan drew us all into a huddled circle and said conspiratorially, 'Now I am trusting all of you not to breathe a word in case a miracle happens. But the chairwoman of the Toadpool Ladies' Charity Guild did whisper to me that the Mystery Celebrity Guest was actually going to be . . .' She left a dramatic pause before declaring triumphantly, 'Archibald Tottingham!'

She waited, but we all kept looking blank.

'Archibald Tottingham!' she repeated.

'You have to hand it to the man,' Dad said. 'He's definitely a Mystery. Who is he?'

Aunt Susan was clearly needled by our ignorance. 'Surely you all remember Archibald Tottingham? He hosted the television series called *Rock Strata in Your Region*!'

'Oh, I remember watching one or two of those,' Mum said. 'As I recall, the programmes were on very, very late at night some of the time Harry was teething.'

'That was so long ago,' my dad said, 'that you can no longer call the man much of a Celebrity.'

'Or, if he isn't coming,' Mum agreed, 'much of a Guest.'

Aunt Susan wasn't pleased with our response. 'I'm not sure everyone would take your flippant and dismissive tone about a man who was, for quite a while, a major public figure.'

'For all of six weeks or so . . .' I heard Dad mutter.

Aunt Susan has sharp ears. 'Quite long enough,' she snapped. 'But he was given the wrong date as well, and they can't even rouse him on the phone.' She dropped her voice to a whisper. 'Indeed, the Ladies fear his absence might tempt more ungenerous souls to put it about that they've been guilty of false advertising. So they're all very keen that no one can claim that they've not put into the lucky dip all the better presents that have been advertised.'

She pointed over the garden fence. Leaning against the sign that said *No parking on the village green* there was a poster, and I must say that some of the prizes drawn on it looked really good. There was a magnifying glass, a bag of crocodile magnets, a fancy new smartphone – even a wind-up nun who spat sparks as she waddled along. That looked quite brilliant! Absolutely brilliant! I knew for certain that I wanted that.

Aunt Susan spread her hands. 'You see my problem? That poster's been displayed in all the villages around here. So if there is no celebrity and nothing but rubbish in the bran tub—'

She didn't finish. But we all knew she thought that that would be the end of any chance she had to make good her bold claim to 'save the day'. And curtains for her chances of being invited to be the next member of the Toadpool Ladies' Charity Guild.

'I don't know what you're going to do about the missing Mystery Celebrity Guest,' said Dad. 'But as regards the presents in the lucky dip, I think you're safe. You have Natasha sitting by the bran tub, and no child in its right mind would ever dare to buy a ticket.'

Everyone stole a glance across the garden at Great-Granny, jabbing her stick as fiercely as she could into the late flowering asters.

Out flew Aunt Susan's neighbour's cat.

ROYAL CONNECTIONS . . .

Aunt Susan made up her mind. Turning to Uncle Tristram, she said decisively, 'Right, then. We'll keep Natasha by the bran tub to stop the bad behaviour. But as for the tickets, I think it would be better if you took charge of selling those as well.'

'As well as what?' he asked.

'As well as the raffle tickets.'

'What raffle tickets?'

'The ones I asked you to come down to sell.'

Uncle Tristram looked even more outraged than he had when I had first suggested that this might be his job. 'Susan, just let me get this straight. You woke me at the crack of dawn and dragged me down here just to sell raffle tickets?'

'You didn't need to get here until two o'clock,' Aunt Susan said defensively.

'But you sent Digby to fetch me! He rang my bell at seven minutes to nine!'

'That's only because I needed him back here to put up the fortune teller's tent.'

Once Uncle Tristram and Aunt Susan start to squabble, they're worse than Harry and me.

'It's not *my* fault you're daft enough to ask Digby to put up a tent.'

'And it's not *my* fault you can't drive because you're in that stupid cast!'

'I'm in this stupid cast because my leg is broken!'

She said contemptuously, 'Your leg can't *still* be broken. That thing's been on for weeks!'

'No longer than is usual. May I remind you that Prince Edward broke his leg on the same day as I did, and I don't hear you scoffing at the fact that he's still in his cast.'

'Prince Edward broke his leg demonstrating to some poor, deprived, inner-city child a subtle move in *polo*!' snapped Aunt Susan. 'His fracture is no doubt a deal more complicated than the sort that people get from being kicked out of their girlfriend's bed for whispering the wrong name.'

My mouth dropped open. 'Is that really how he broke his leg?'

Aunt Susan started in on me. 'For heaven's sake, Ralph! Don't you read the papers?'

Now mightily confused, I turned to Uncle Tristram. 'I didn't know that you were in the papers!'

'Not him,' Aunt Susan corrected irritably. 'Edward!'

'Oh, so it's "Edward" now, is it?' Uncle Tristram scoffed. 'All pally, are we?' And we all sniggered quietly behind our hands because Aunt Susan can't forget that she once had tea at a house where Princess Anne was rumoured to have popped in earlier, and was said to be possibly coming back later.

Aunt Susan wasn't giving up. She just put on a most mysterious look and murmured, 'Let us just say that there are one or two royal connections . . .'

'Royal connections!' jeered Uncle Tristram. 'Oh, yes? Like *which*?'

Aunt Susan tossed her head. 'Tristram, I think you'll find that people who move in the same social circles as the royal family tend to try not to gossip.'

Rather than risk another blast of derision, she hurried off.

'That leaves me as the only one without a job,' Mum said. 'Does that mean I'm to be the fortune teller?'

'You can't be a frightfully good one,' Harry informed her, 'if you don't yet *know*.'

THE PRINCIPLES OF COMMUNISM

Harry went onto the front lawn to practise on his flowerpots, and Dad rushed off to rescue some poor creature that Great-Granny had trapped beneath the lobelias. That left Uncle Tristram and me alone together. I offered him a boiled sweet. He peered at it closely as he picked off the fluff. 'Is this one of Dora's? Then I will. They're very good.'

We sucked together for a while, and then my uncle cheered up enough to say, 'Oh, well.

We must look on the bright side. I've always wanted to take charge of a prize raffle. It seems to me that there is something very foolish and wrong about the way they're usually organized.'

'I always thought they were quite clever,' I confessed. 'Those little books of tickets, all with a tear-off bit to match that gets dropped in the bucket.'

'That,' he said scornfully, 'is the sort of thing a chimpanzee could work out for itself.'

'Well,' I insisted, 'at least you have to admit that raffles are fair.'

'Fair?'

'Yes. The more tickets you can afford to buy, the greater your chance of a prize.'

He spread his hands. 'That is my point entirely! Once again, the rich come out on top. Here is a raffle – the perfect opportunity for a painless bit of Redistribution of Wealth – and it is thrown away. Utterly wasted!'

I must admit that I was mystified. 'What's "Redistribution of Wealth"?'

Uncle Tristram let out a snort of contempt. 'Lord's sake, Ralph! Haven't you ever read Friedrich Engels' ground-breaking masterpiece, *The Principles of Communism*?'

I glared at him. I'd had enough. First I'm

ticked off by Aunt Susan for not keeping up with all the royal gossip in the newspapers. Then I'm ticked off by Uncle Tristram for not ploughing through great heavy volumes about running raffles. For the first time in my life I reckoned there might be some sort of family resemblance between my favourite uncle and his bossy sister.

Annoyed, I turned my back without another word and set off for the house, deliberately going as fast as I could without actually running, to leave him *scrunch-scrunch, scrunch-scrunching* along on his leg cast, falling further and further behind me.

SWAP?

On the lawn, Harry was practising walking round and round the sundial on the plastic flowerpots. I offered him a boiled sweet.

'Are they from Dora?' He reached out to pat the bulge in my side pocket. 'You got a lot. Smart work!'

'Take two,' I said. Then, pointing at the flowerpots, I asked him, more in desperate hope than any expectation, 'Swap?'

He nodded at the dishrag trailing from my other pocket. 'What, for the wear-an-old-leotard-of-Mum's job? You must be joking!'

'They'll laugh at you as well,' I warned. 'Probably just as much. Because they'll all know that those flowerpot things are made for toddlers.'

'Maybe they will,' he said, and grinned. 'But at least, while they're doing it, I shall be wearing proper *trousers*.'

I stuck my tongue out and went into the house.

YOU'RE GOING TO TELL FORTUNES!

Mum wasn't in the kitchen. When I peered round the door I saw that Aunt Susan was alone in there, fighting her espresso machine. (Dad says that every drink it makes tastes like stewed carpet, and even Mum admits that if it's a choice between one of her sister's coffees and a cup of warm mud, she'd pick the mud.)

I was about to ask where Mum had gone when the machine went berserk. And by the time its vicious splutterings damped down, I had already heard behind me the sound of cursing in a voice I recognized.

I turned to track the grumbling up the stairs, and crept along the landing. I was determined to corner Mum and force her to admit that the plan was bats: there was no way that I could wear her stupid leotard and do this show. So, dangling the horrid thing in front of me, I pushed at the half-open door of Aunt Susan's bedroom, where Mum was struggling into a giant blouse covered in huge, bright, look!-we-did-paints-today-at-nursery swirls.

I thought I'd start off trying to be pleasant. 'That's very pretty.'

Mum's voice came out all muffled and sarcastic. 'Think so? Myself, I found the words "designer bag lady" sprang to mind.'

I find it's better not to back down too fast after a compliment, or they suspect you didn't mean what you said. So I persisted. 'But it is covered with nice embroidery.'

'To those, like you, who think the Tattooed Man looks fetching, the pattern must work a treat.'

Talk about rude and ratty! I gave up. 'Well, if you hate the thing so much, why are you trying it on?'

She told me irritably, 'I am not "trying it on", Ralph. There would be no point. The thing will never fit me for the simple reason that I'm not an elephant.'

'What are you doing, then?'

Mum sighed at me as if I were a halfwit. 'I'm simply trying to work out which side's the front of it, and which is the back.'

I glanced across at the bed, on which lay a massive flowery skirt and an embroidered headscarf studded with gold coins. 'So you were right! You're going to tell the fortunes!'

'Amazing prescience!' she said sardonically. 'Why, you could do the job yourself.'

I'm used to being teased by Mum. I just ignore it. In any case, another thought had struck me. 'But you'll be making all the fortunes up.'

'Like every soothsayer in the world,' Mum scoffed.

That disappointed me. I'd thought that some of them, at least, had second sight. 'Surely,' I said to her, 'you're not going to try to tell me that every single fortune teller who ever lived was just a fake?'

She turned away from me with her I-am-not-wasting-one-more-microsecond-of-my-short-life-on-this-conversation look. I pointed to the newspaper on Aunt Susan's bedside table. 'What about horoscopes?'

'What *about* horoscopes?' Cracking, Mum reached across to pick up the paper. I watched her flick through till she found a section called *Lady Leila's Stargazing Predictions*. Her eyes ran down the columns, then she challenged me: 'So you'd read this, and you'd be daft enough to believe that everybody in the entire world born between August the twenty-fourth and September the twenty-third—'

'That's every Virgo like me!'

Mum totally ignored me. '– is in line for a windfall.'

I reached out for the paper. 'Ace! Is that what it says?'

Mum was exasperated. 'Ralph! For heaven's sake! Surely you don't waste time reading these idiotic things!'

You can't win, can you? Half the time you're

being nagged because you don't read things; the other half you're being nagged because you do.

A TAX ON THE STUPID

I steered us back to safer ground. 'Well, if you're going to be the fortune teller, how are you going to decide what to tell people?'

'The usual way. I'm going to size up my clients as they come in. I'll take a stab at guessing what they're like, then I'll say something suitable.'

'Like what?'

Mum pulled the skirt on over her jeans and reached into a drawer for some pins. 'Well, if some spruce old colonel comes in wearing freshly polished shoes, and with the few white hairs that he has left combed neatly in a parting, then I might look into my crystal ball and tell him he's the sort of chap who likes things orderly.'

'And?'

She thought some more. 'And, though he gets on well enough with other people, sometimes their sheer untidiness and sloppiness gets on his nerves.' She nodded briskly.

'That sort of thing should do the trick.'

'And what if it's some scruffy lady who has toast crumbs down her front and tatty sneakers?'

'I'll say the crystal ball tells me she's very arty and individual, but people like her all the more for that.'

'And when they ask about the future?'

Mum jerked a thumb towards the newspaper. 'I'll do what Lady Leila does and keep it airy-fairy and bland.'

'So if you tell them they're in line for a windfall—'

'For heaven's sake, Ralph! It's a rare week when no one hands you anything, if only some old jar of jam that they don't want.' She clipped on the loopy gold earrings. 'Anyone soft enough to pay good money to a fortune teller will surely manage to convince themselves there was some truth in what was said.'

I asked her virtuously, 'Isn't that rather dishonest?' (I was a bit cheesed off about the windfall I'd just lost.)

'Nonsense,' said Mum. 'It's just a tax on the stupid. And in this case a good one, since the proceeds go to charity.'

I scoured my brain for Uncle Tristram's fancy words. 'I see,' I said. 'The perfect opportunity for a painless bit of Redistribution of Wealth.'

Mum's mouth dropped open. I would have liked to walk out then, leaving her staring. But I was there for a reason. 'Mum, about this leotard . . .'

She cast a glance towards the droopy rag that I held out towards her. 'Yes? What about it?'

'Well, I can't wear it. I would look ridiculous.'

She waved a hand over the blouse and skirt. 'And you think that I don't?'

'I'd rather wear your gear than mine. I'm more than happy to swap. Then I can tell the fortunes that aren't fortunes after all, and you can do the trapeze act.'

'How can I do the trapeze act? You know I only have to glance at a toddler sitting on a swing and I feel nauseous.' She saw my face, and showed a spark of pity. 'You could ask Titania.'

'But she's already doing the poetry recitation and the pixie song.'

'Why would that worry her? Your cousin spends her whole life practising her various stage skills. I would imagine she'd enjoy displaying one more.'

I felt quite cheered. 'All right. I'll ask Titania.'

Mum turned back to the mirror and pulled on the headscarf with the dangling golden coins. 'Yes, do. I can't imagine anything stopping her saying yes.'

'You're right,' I said, completely confident. (It's not for nothing that Harry and I privately call Titania the Great Big Fancy Show-Off.) 'Neither can I.'

I GET THICK WHEN I'M UPTHIDE DOWN

I found Titania on the top step outside the kitchen door, singing a song to a pumpkin. She broke off, startled, as I sat down beside her. 'Oh! Hi, Ralph. Nithe rabbit thlipperth.'

'Thank you.' I had good reason to be polite. 'Don't let me stop you singing to your vegetable.'

She looked at me as if I were the mad one, so I changed tack and offered her a boiled sweet.

'No, thankth,' she said. 'I don't eat thweetth in cathe I get cavitieth.'

I looked around but her mother was nowhere in sight. Titania meant it. So I put the boiled sweet back in my pocket. 'Listen,' I said.

'You know you're really, really good at shows and dancing and stuff.'

'Yeth,' she said (rather complacently, I thought).

I laid it on with a trowel. 'And everyone thinks that everything you do on stage is absolutely wonderful.'

She nodded. 'Yeth.'

'Well, I've a brilliant idea. I thought that you could take on one more thing, just to please everybody even more.'

She couldn't have looked more eager. 'What?'

'Do the trapeze act.'

Titania shook her head regretfully. 'Thorry. I get thick when I'm upthide down.'

I skipped the obvious joke.

'What, really sick? Throw-up sick?'

'Yeth.'

'I didn't know that.' I thought back to the million boring shows Titania has put on for us over the years. 'In fact, I've seen you upside down plenty of times.'

'That wath before.'

'Before what?'

'Before I fell on my bottom and one or two people in the front row were mean enough to thnigger.'

'Snigger?' I felt a horrid pang of guilt.

'Really?'

'Yeth. It wath horrible. Thtupid and rude! And I know that it oughtn't to make a differenth. But it hath.'

'What, like a sort of curse?'

She shrugged. 'I thuppose tho. All I know ith that every time I go upthide down on thtage now, I throw up.'

'Oh, right.' And suddenly I felt really uneasy. Jerking my feet from side to side to make my rabbits' ears flap, I tried to think things through. After all, even if I was hurl-your-popcorn-at-me rubbish on the trapeze, I still wouldn't throw up over the audience. And if it was my fault (and Harry's) that this weird nervous sickness happened to Titania, then maybe I deserved to have to make a fool of myself, and be sniggered at in turn.

Titania interrupted my musings. 'What are you wearing for your trapethe act?'

I held the leotard up in front of her. 'Mum says I should wear this.'

She tipped her head to one side, studying it critically. 'That lookth a bit like a dead thlug.'

There wasn't any arguing with that, so I kept quiet.

'And you'll look like a dead thlug too, when you are wearing it.'

'Yes,' I agreed.

She reached out to poke it dubiously. 'Would you like me to fixth it?'

'Fix it?'

'Make it fit better,' she said. 'Brighten it up. And put on a thpangle or two.'

Any port in a storm, I thought. At least spangles might distract the audience from noticing that the leotard was dangling round my knees. So, 'Yes,' I told her, 'thpangles would be good.'

She looked at me with deep suspicion. 'Ralph, are you teathing me?'

I realized what I'd said. 'No, not at all! When I said thpangles I meant spangles. It just came out wrong.'

You have to hand it to Titania: she might like showing off, but she is generous by nature. Easy to appease. 'All right,' she said, and led me into the house. I followed her upstairs to her room. She went straight in, but I was distracted by a large cardboard box that lay half open by the door with something huge and black and hairy curled up inside it.

'What's this?'

She glanced back. 'That ith my Wumpy boxth.'

I was still nervous. 'Does it bite?'

She came across to see what I was looking at, then reached down to pick the black and hairy thing out of the carton.

It fell in ripples.

'Oh, I see!'

It was just one of those three brilliant beards that Uncle Tristram gave us all the Christmas before. ('Proof,' my dad muttered, 'that the man is mad.') Harry and I thought they were the best presents ever. Mine had been torn to shreds by Albert's dog. ('It serves you right,' said Mum, 'for using it to tease poor Pongo.') And Harry had lost his on a Scouts field trip somewhere near Berwick-upon-Tweed.

'How did you keep your beard so clean and tidy?' I asked Titania, fascinated.

My cousin shrugged. 'I almotht never wear it. I only put it in there to keep the dutht off my collection.'

She tipped the box. Out fell a hundred droopy knitted weirdo animals with soulful button eyes.

I stared at them. 'What are these? Knitted zombies?'

'No,' she said proudly. 'Wumpieth. I invented them and then I made them.'

I was astonished. 'You made all of these?'

'Yeth. I've been crocheting them for weekth and weekth, and Mummy'th going to thell them all thith afternoon.'

Fat chance! I thought. But I said nothing, just bent down to help her shovel all the Wumpies back in the box. Then I looked around. Titania's room had changed a lot since I was last sent up to sit in it for picking my nose at the table. Back then it had a really fancy wallpaper of baby bears peeping out from behind trees. It was like being in a busy forest clearing. Now the whole room was violet – walls, ceiling, curtains, duvet – even the carpet. And swooping and pirouetting across the walls were dozens of hand-painted silver fairies, all sprinkling glitter from their wands.

'They're good,' I had to admit. 'Who painted those?'

'I did,' she said, 'when I was poorly and off thchool.'

I can't imagine being allowed to stay home long enough to paint a single door knob, let alone fairies on walls. 'What did you have, for heaven's sake?'

I waited, half expecting her to answer, 'Leprosy' or 'The Black Death'. But all she said was, 'An attack of the thniffles.'

I couldn't believe my ears. 'What – like a *cold*?' (Nobody's *ever* let me stay off school for something as feeble as a cold. And even when the teachers have taken one quick look at me and sent me straight back home, I have been made to spend the day wiping down cabinets or cleaning shoes.)

'*Nearly* a cold,' boasted Titania. 'But thtaying home wath the right thing to do becauthe it fended it off.'

Not even wanting to think about the sheer unfairness of life, I shoved the leotard into her arms. She held it out, all drab and sagging. 'I'm not just thinking thpangles,' she admitted. 'But maybe pompomth ath well.'

'I am not wearing pompoms! Pompoms are for *girls*.'

'What about glitter?'

I will admit I've always had a bit of a soft spot for glitter. 'Maybe,' I said. 'So long as it's not pink.'

'Purple?'

Now I was cracking fast. 'Purple's all right, I suppose.'

'What about thtars?'

'Stars?' I considered. Stars are a little girly. But sorcerers have them on their pointy hats. 'I'm fine with stars, so long as I can have some moons as well.'

'I've got moonth.' Titania pulled out the top drawer in a little wooden cabinet under her window. Inside were heaps of silver crescent moons.

'Hey! They're good! What else have you got in there?'

Titania slid out one drawer after another. It was a treasure trove. She had jewels, feathers, beads and coloured strings, frogging and braids and ribbons – everything you might need to make a dingy leotard stop the show.

I couldn't help it. I said, 'Brilliant!'

'You can help decorate it if you want.'

I was so tempted. All that glittery stuff. But then I thought about the audience watching me glisten and flash, but me still not being able even to thread my legs through properly. It would be even more embarrassing than falling on a lump of chewing gum and ending up showing a flash of bottom.

'No,' I said with regret. 'I think it would be better for me to spend the time practising.'

'I thuppothe it would.' But I think Titania realized how much I envied her amazing stuff because, as I was leaving, she held out the Christmas beard. 'Do you want thith? Becauthe I won't be needing it after today.'

Did I want another brilliant, bushy, four-foot-long, send-the-neighbours'-dog-entirely-wild, tickly, have-a-laugh-in-school, black, not-yet-tangled-up Rasputin beard?

Why would she even *ask* me?

Do camels *spit*?

IS IT A MURDER YOU'RE PLANNING?

On my way back through the kitchen, I came across Uncle Tristram pulling one evil-looking knife after another out of a drawer and testing them gingerly against his thumb.

I stopped. 'Is it a *murder* you're planning?'

He looked a little startled. 'No. Why do you ask?'

I shrugged. 'Only because, if it was, I think I would be voting for you to kill Great-Granny.'

He looked around nervously. 'Is she inside? I thought she was still out in the garden, tormenting next door's cat and mashing the late flowering asters.'

'Unless she's slipped off through her Private Portal.'

Uncle Tristram looked mystified. 'What Private Portal?'

'The one to Hell.'

He stared at me. Then he reached out to lay his hand on my forehead. 'Funny. You don't seem feverish. Perhaps it's the start of a brain tumour making you say such odd things.'

'I like that! You're the one who's creeping around somebody else's kitchen clutching a dangerous weapon.'

He held the knife up. 'This? I'm just borrowing it.'

'So you're not going to murder anyone – even Great-Granny?'

'Of course I'm not. I'm just bored. And then I saw this pumpkin lying about on the back step—'

'I think that pumpkin is Titania's pet.'

'Her pet? Titania has pet *vegetables*?'

'Well,' I said, losing confidence in the idea. 'All I can say is that I heard her singing a song to that pumpkin.'

Uncle Tristram's face cleared. 'But that doesn't mean a thing. Titania would sing to a telegraph pole if there was nothing else standing about.' He grasped the knife more firmly. 'No, Titania won't care. And there's still plenty of time before I have to do anything about these raffle tickets.'

'I'd help you,' I said wistfully, 'except I have to work up my trapeze skills.'

'I know!' he said. 'Sit on Titania's swing, then you can keep me company while I help you plan your act.'

'All right.' I hitched myself up onto the swing and watched while Uncle Tristram stuck out his leg cast to lower himself onto the back door step. He took the knife to the pumpkin and started just like everyone does on Halloween, cutting a zigzag line all round the top.

I leaned way back. 'Should I take off my slippers?'

'No, no,' said Uncle Tristram. 'People are fond of rabbits. They'll add a homely touch of style to the performance.'

'Righty-ho.'

I worked my way up into a good swing, and stuck my legs out sideways.

'Elegant,' encouraged Uncle Tristram. 'An excellent start.'

I did my imitation of Titania. 'Are you *teathing* me, Uncle Trithtram?'

We shared a chuckle as he lifted the lid off his pumpkin and started scooping out the flesh. I worked myself up higher, but it was hard to concentrate while I was watching my uncle dip his hands inside the pumpkin shell over and over to pull out handfuls of stringy orange flesh and slimy seeds, and dump them beside him on the back step.

'That looks *disgusting*.'

'Doesn't it just!' He took another look at what I was doing. 'Can you hang upside down and thread your legs through?'

'Sometimes,' I said. 'And sometimes I get stuck.'

'I'm not surprised, wearing those trousers. What you need is a showman's leotard.'

He'd said the word without collapsing in sniggers. So, 'It's on its way,' I admitted. 'Titania's busy making it look a bit less like a dead slug.'

I pulled myself up into a standing position,

and had a go at one or two fancy threadings-in-and-out.

'That's good,' he said. 'Now try a proper somersault.'

'What, holding the ropes?'

'Yes. Just pretend you're standing on the ground, then flip yourself over.'

I gave it a go. It burned my palms a little, but it worked.

'Flip yourself back,' he ordered.

Back I flipped.

'You're not too bad at all,' he told me. 'Try a bit of fancy-shmancy swinging, sticking your legs out all over.'

I did that quite successfully.

'Now try the same things standing up again.'

So I did that.

'Frankly,' he said, 'I think you're well on the way to doing a good job.'

'And so are you,' I said. For all the time that I'd been following orders, Uncle Tristram had been scooping out the pumpkin. Now he began on its face. I took a little rest, watching with interest as he hacked away.

'Those eye-holes look a bit wobbly and uneven-looking,' I couldn't help remarking.

'Well, there you go,' said Uncle Tristram.

'This pumpkin's had a heavy night and isn't feeling too well.'

He started on the mouth, making it look turned down and truly enormous.

'He looks unhappy.'

'And so would you, if you'd drunk as much as this pumpkin.'

Instead of carving one triangular hole for the nose, Uncle Tristram bored two little round ones.

'I've never seen a pumpkin with real nostrils before.'

'Doubt if you've seen one throwing up, either.' Reaching behind him, Uncle Tristram scooped up a handful of the disgusting stringy stuff tangled with seeds, and dropped it back in the pumpkin shell till it was dripping out through the nose and pouring out of the mouth. 'What do you think?'

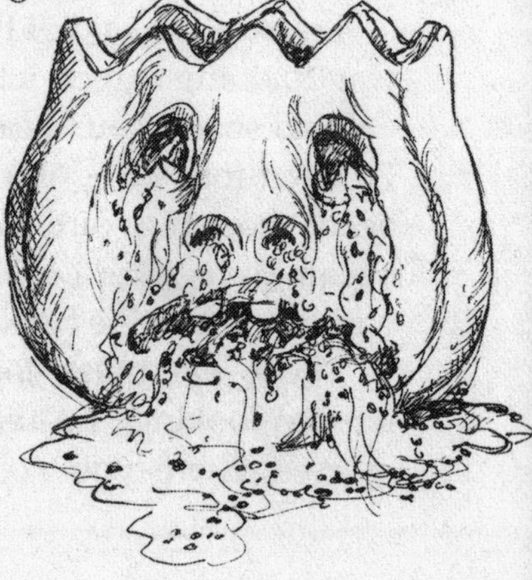

I was delighted with it. 'Only the finest pumpkin I've ever seen!'

'It is good, isn't it?'

'Revolting!'

Uncle Tristram leaned back, satisfied. 'Yes, something of a triumph. It'll look very good indeed, a bit more shrivelled in a month or so, on my doorstep on Halloween.' He rose laboriously to his feet, brushing a few stray slimy orange strings off his cast. Then he inspected the knife blade. 'For heaven's sake!' he said. 'This is already blunt. I think I'll nip inside and swap it for another before we go looking for more of Titania's pets.' A glint came into his eyes. 'Or we could even revert to *your* plan.'

I wasn't quite sure what he meant. 'Which plan was that?'

He stared at me. 'You must remember! *Murder!*'

MY, THEY LOOK NASTY

'*Murder?*'

We turned to see Dad struggling through the side gate, pushing what looked like a flag pole stuck on half a bike.

'What's that?'

He sighed. 'What does it look like, Ralph?'

I told him, 'It looks like a flagpole stuck on half a bike.'

'Well, it's an old unicycle,' he declared. 'Your Uncle Digby found it in the village hall store cupboard, underneath the trapeze, and your Aunt Susan has insisted I try to master it before the show.'

'Really?' I said. (Up until then, I'd thought that I was the unlucky one, having to work on my trapeze skills.)

Uncle Tristram lurched over to help Dad through the gate. 'Blimey!' he couldn't help saying. 'That thing is taller than I am. I wouldn't want to fall off that!'

'No,' Dad said tartly, raising a trouser leg to show us his brand-new bruises. 'No, you certainly wouldn't.'

To cheer him up, I offered him a boiled sweet.

'Dora's?' he asked. 'Yes, don't mind if I do.'

We sucked together as Uncle Tristram stared at the unicycle. 'Pretty impressive, though,' he said to Dad admiringly, 'even for you to manage to get up on it in the first place.'

'I haven't,' Dad confessed. 'You might think it's impossible to fall off something that you haven't yet managed to get on. But I have done that several times.'

We all tipped back our heads to gaze at the saddle on top. It looked as tiny, far away and unreachable as some baby eaglet in a mountain nest.

I pointed to the back door steps. 'You could try climbing onto it from there.'

'Exactly where I was headed,' Dad said irritably, 'when I came across the two of you discussing murder.'

On his way over there, he stepped into the heap of slime and seeds.

'Hey!' Uncle Tristram warned him. 'Watch where you're putting your feet. That is our precious pumpkin sick you're kicking all over the place.'

Dad leaned the unicycle against the wall and stepped back, pointing at the knife that Uncle Tristram had dropped on the grass. 'Is this the murder weapon? Whom did you have in mind? I certainly hope it's Aunt Susan, for roping us into all this in the first place.'

'Actually,' I told him, 'I think Great-Granny is the first in the queue.'

'Oh, fair enough,' said Dad. 'Though I do hope the pair of you won't rule out doing everyone a favour with one of those generous "two-for-one" offers.'

Plonking himself down heavily on the steps, he pulled up the other trouser leg. The bruises on that side were even worse.

'My, they look nasty,' Uncle Tristram said, inspecting them. 'Why don't you give up on the whole idea of riding that thing? You'll never learn to do it properly before the show.'

'Oh, yes?' said Dad. 'Bale out, and run the risk of Susan killing me before you two get round to murdering her?'

I do try to be helpful. 'We could swap the murdering order round, and do Aunt Susan first.'

Nobody paid my suggestion the slightest attention.

'I have an idea,' Uncle Tristram said. 'Go on stage holding the unicycle as if you were about to leap on it and impress the audience with your skills. But then, as soon as you're standing out there in front of them, do something else instead.'

We watched Dad think about the idea while testing his bruises with his fingertips. Finally, he raised his head, looking a little more hopeful. 'I *could* try that, couldn't I? I could come out pretending that I was going to ride the thing, then act as if I always started off by telling a joke. They'll laugh, and then I could pretend that I was trying to please them by telling them another. I could go on and on like that till my time's up.'

'That's right,' said Uncle Tristram. 'Keep up the jokes, and then look at your watch and act astonished.'

Dad was quite keen now. 'Then I could trail off stage looking quite disappointed, as if I'd accidentally missed my chance to show the audience my brilliant circus skills.'

'Excellent scheme!' said Uncle Tristram. 'Which joke will you tell first?'

Dad scoured his brain. 'There's one I know about three robbers who are being chased by the police.'

'Yes, I've heard that one,' Uncle Tristram said.

'I haven't,' I complained. 'I heard three quarters of it early this morning when we were having breakfast. But Dad never got to the end.'

They both ignored me again.

'Yes, that one about the robbers will do nicely. Then what about the one about the piece of string who went into a café to buy a drink?'

'Good one!' Dad chortled. 'Then I could finish up with that great joke about the talking centipede.'

They shared a laugh over the memory of that while I sat sulking. Finally Dad turned my way. 'No time to sit there growing mildew on your rabbit slippers,' he warned. 'You only have a short time left to practise your own part of the show.'

'I like that!' I was outraged. 'You wriggle out of doing your bit properly, and still expect me to do mine! And in a *leotard*!'

But for the third time in a row, the two of them simply ignored me.

THORRY! I MEANT THPANGLES!

I left Uncle Tristram sneaking Aunt Susan's ruined knife back into the kitchen drawer. What Dad had said about not having much more time before the show had made me nervous, and I went off to find the real trapeze so I could practise on that.

On the way over the front lawn I found Harry twirling on his flowerpots.

'Swap?' I asked once again, and added temptingly, 'Titania's busy turning the leotard into something really special.'

He sneered at me. 'What, painting fairies on it?'

'No!'

'Sticking on glitter and spangles – whoops! Thorry! I mean thpangles!'

'You're being really mean,' I said. 'And I

shall laugh when you fall off your flowerpots.'

He did a fancy flowerpot twirl. 'Fat chance! I'm going to practise jumping on them next. That'll make everyone stare.'

'Yes,' I said. 'At the biggest toddler on the block.' And I strode off.

DID I HEAR SCREAMING?

It wasn't safe to go through the side gate because Great-Granny was in front of it, prodding some insolent lump of soil and ticking off songbirds for cheek. So I went down the drive and walked along the verge. On my way up the path into the village hall I had to pick my way round the fortune teller's tent that Uncle Digby was still putting up. He wasn't doing very well. The sides were flapping and the tent was leaning horribly.

'It's not the easiest thing,' I heard him muttering as I went by.

I tried to comfort him. 'Look on the bright side. All that flapping of the sides makes it look haunted.'

That cheered him up. He stepped back to admire his handiwork. 'Yes. Leaving it tipping over in that way is probably a good idea.

Makes it look like a witch's hat.'

'I think so too,' I said, and went past into the hall. I found the real trapeze set up on stage. It didn't look too high until I tried to scramble up on it. I had to borrow one of the chairs the Toadpool Ladies' Charity Guild had put out for the audience, and even with that underneath it was a bit of a jump.

It took a deal of nervous shuffling before I even got myself facing the front with each hand on a rope. Then, very gingerly, I started to swing. Even before I started, the stage beneath me looked horribly far away, and the hall even further. I worked myself up higher and the bar that I was sitting on swung out into thin air. I clenched my eyes shut. My heart pumped. I heard the rush of blood inside my ears.

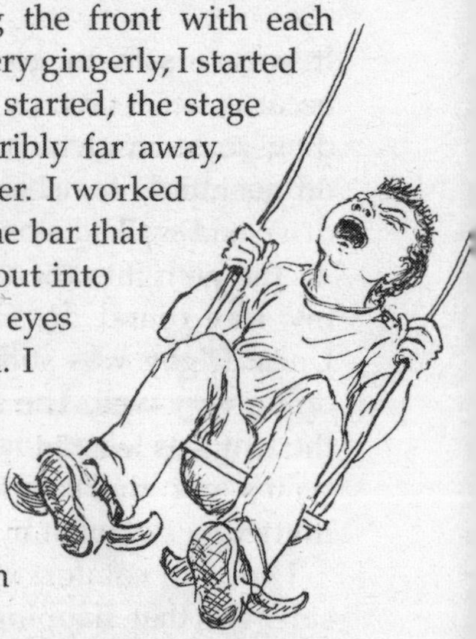

It took for ever till the swing came to a halt, and I dared open my eyes.

Uncle Tristram was standing at the back of the hall. 'Did I hear *screaming*? Was it you?'

'No,' I said faintly, not even making much of a stab at trying to sound truthful.

'What are you doing up there if you've no head for heights?'

'I didn't know I didn't.' I gathered my wits enough to get irritable. 'Nobody's ever forced me to risk my life on anything so dangerous before.'

'Can you get down by yourself?'

'No,' I admitted, so Uncle Tristram made his way past the rows of chairs and hobbled up the steps. Anchoring his cast on the stage, he reached up to put his hands firmly round my middle. We stayed like that until he got impatient and said, 'Ralph, you will have to let go of the ropes or we'll be here for ever.'

'I'm *trying*.'

'Let go right now. Or *I* shall.'

I let go, fast.

'That's better.'

I clamped my arms round his neck while he lifted me down. My knees were wobbling so much I couldn't stand, so we sat on the front of the stage, waiting for me to feel better.

THE MOUNTFIELD FAMILY CURSE

Uncle Tristram reached down to brush a few last slimy pumpkin strands off his leg cast and flick away the odd seed. 'Well, well,' he said. 'I see that you have been struck down as well.'

'Struck down?'

'By the Mountfield Family Curse.'

It rang a bell. 'You mean that business Dad complained about of people forever ruining our Sundays with interruptions and demands, and having to go places?'

'No, not that one,' he said. 'The weird "no confidence" thing. When we were young, your mother used to spend as much time hanging upside down as any fruit bat. She married James Mountfield and – poof! – now she can't look at a toddler on a swing without feeling nauseous.'

'What do you think it is?'

'Well,' he said darkly, 'I suspect that it's to do with your great-grandmother.' He peered at me with interest. 'Did you by any chance annoy her on the journey down?'

I thought about her calling me a bucket-head. And saying that I had a brain so empty that the doors in it banged in the wind. She'd called me and Harry lunatics and idiot articles. She'd warned me to watch my fat lip, and threatened to rip off my hand and chew it in front of me.

'No, nothing special,' I said. 'No worse than

usual, anyway.'

'Strange,' he said. 'Because there is a body of opinion that thinks that one of your great-granny's hobbies is making members of your family feel sick.'

'You mean she actually puts *spells* on people?'

'No, no,' he said. 'More like a sort of general ill-willing.'

'Ill-willing?'

'Yes. Like voodoo. No one can quite explain what's happening, or why. But still your health begins to slip away. The Mountfield Family Curse is like that, but with people's confidence.' He gazed up innocently towards the rafters. 'And now, of course, the curse is clearly spreading wider – to anyone who spends a lot of time around your family.' He shot me an unnervingly keen look. 'You take Titania, for example. Up until recently she could do the most splendid things – cartwheels and somersaults, handstands, back flips. And then what happens? She tumbles on stage and some silly and insensitive person in the audience chooses to *snigger*. And now Titania can't even perform her Dance of the Baby Daffodil. If she so much as bends her stalk in the breeze, she has to clutch her stomach and rush off the stage.'

'She's that bad?'

'I'm afraid she is.'

I was still staring guiltily at the floor when a door banged. Aunt Susan suddenly appeared at the back of the hall, clutching a clipboard. 'Lunch time!' she called out briskly. 'I'm taking orders for your sandwiches.'

'Pastrami on a bed of rocket, please,' said Uncle Tristram. 'With avocado and Roquefort, sprinkled with pine nuts toasted in walnut oil, all on Italian wholemeal bread, perhaps with the teensiest smear of freshly crushed basil.'

I watched Aunt Susan scribble all that down. She raised her head. 'What about you, Ralph?'

'Cheese, please.'

My uncle looked at me, clearly both pained and startled. 'Just cheese? Surely you want to pep it up with onion or tomato?'

'Just cheese is fine.'

He was still fretting. 'But what *sort* of cheese?'

'Any sort.'

'At least try the new Vignotte!'

I shrugged. But there was no point anyway, because Aunt Susan had gone. We turned our attention back to the problem in hand. 'If I can't manage the trapeze, what am I going to do? Harry won't swap.'

'But there are other things that you could do.'

'Like what?'

'Sell raffle tickets?'

I saw his little game. 'While you slope off to chat up girls all afternoon?'

Again he stared up at the rafters. 'Possibly. As a reward for my negotiating skills.'

That sounded like a bargain. 'You'd actually dare to tell Aunt Susan I am copping out? You *promise*?'

'I'll make it clear to her that you're the latest victim of the Mountfield Family Curse, and it's impossible for you to even *look* at a trapeze ever again.'

'She won't be pleased to see another of the things on the poster go – what with her not having any Mystery Celebrity Guest.'

'Ah, well,' he said. 'If I am honest, I still harbour hopes in that direction.'

I didn't argue. My knees had finally stopped trembling and I thought it only fair to warn Titania that, if Uncle Tristram kept his promise, I might no longer need the leotard. So we went back. As we were crossing the green, Uncle Tristram stopped for a moment and innocently asked the side of the fortune-telling tent that was still thrashing about most horribly,

'Coming for lunch, Digby?'

We heard the muffled reply. 'Tell Susan I'll be with you in two ticks. This is a tad more tricky than hanging that old trapeze from the stage beam. But still, I think I've got it sorted, finally.'

'I'm sure you have,' said Uncle Tristram. And we hurried on, so Uncle Digby wouldn't hear us sniggering.

SWAP?

On my way back across the lawn I saw Harry jumping on his flowerpots and peeled off to ask him, almost out of habit, 'Swap?'

'Dream on!' he chortled back.

'You should be careful,' I warned. 'Those things are only plastic. They weren't designed to take your weight. You'll probably end up splitting them down the sides, and when you give them back to Albert he'll bite you. Very hard. And I shall laugh.'

He grinned. 'Not half as loudly as I'll be laughing when you're up on stage wearing that sluggy leotard.'

(I couldn't blame him. I'd have said the same.)

I WILL KILL AGAIN!

I caught up with Uncle Tristram, who had stopped at the back door to push a trickle of stray pumpkin vomit back towards the mouth. 'How did it go?' he asked me sympathetically. 'Any luck with the Flowerpot Hog?'

'No,' I said sourly.

'Too bad. It's not your day at all.'

And I thought he was right. But he had troubles of his own to face. As we went up the back steps, we heard Aunt Susan going mad inside the kitchen. 'My knife! Who's been at my best knife?'

'Whoops!' Uncle Tristram said, hastily backing away. He led me round to the front door and we crept down the hall towards the telly room. After a minute or two, my dad crept in as well. 'Aha! So this is where you two are hiding! Mind if I join you?' He nodded back towards the kitchen. 'I must say, things are getting pretty hot in there.'

'Nothing to do with me,' said Uncle Tristram. But you could tell he was nervous. A moment later, we were hearing more screams – this time from Titania. 'My pumpkin! Look at my pumpkin!

See its face! Oh, it looks horrible! *Horrible!*'

'Ungrateful child,' my uncle murmured. But I did notice that he shrank more deeply into the armchair, as if he hoped to vanish out of sight.

In stormed Aunt Susan, brandishing the knife we took to be no longer at its best. 'This is *your* doing, isn't it, Tristram? Confess! Confess! You took my very best and most expensive knife, and you've played havoc with it!'

He tried to defend himself. 'I merely scraped it once or twice along the doorstep, trying to sharpen it.'

'The blade's completely ruined! This knife is *useless*.'

Dad stepped in. 'I doubt that, Susan. Hand it over here. I'll bet it's still sharp enough to cut your brother's throat.'

Aunt Susan's eyes still flashed with rage. 'Fine by me! Absolutely fine! He would deserve it!'

'Hey, steady on!' warned Uncle Tristram. 'All I did was—'

But she'd stormed out, still brandishing the knife. Dad turned to Uncle Tristram. 'Why do you get your sister into such a bate?' he asked with amiable interest. 'Why do you do that every single time you come into this house?'

'Not *every* time,' said Uncle Tristram sulkily.

'Yes, *every* time,' Dad told him firmly. 'Right from the day when Susan and Digby moved to Upper Toadpool and started on Titania's nursery.'

'That was a *joke*!' insisted Uncle Tristram.

'What was a joke?' I asked him, curious.

'Nothing!' he said. 'A tiny scribble on the wall, that's all. And then, almost at once, I pasted that stupid Bears-in-the-Forest wallpaper over it and covered it up.'

'Without warning anyone!' Dad challenged him.

Uncle Tristram scowled. 'Well, how was I to know that they were going to redecorate the nursery before Titania was old enough to take a joke?'

'A *joke*?' said Dad. 'You think it's amusing for a child to be left for a few minutes in her own bedroom, happily peeling off old wallpaper, only to come across a message like that scrawled on the plaster underneath in blood-red paint?'

'I thought it was funny,' muttered Uncle Tristram.

'The message, "**I WILL KILL AGAIN!**"? *Funny?*' Shaking his head in despair, Dad prised himself out of his chair and left the room.

I turned to Uncle Tristram. We stared at one

another for a moment or two in silence. And then we took to sniggering again, twenty times worse.

A BYWORD FOR FOOLISHNESS

The merriment didn't last. Two minutes later Dad called the two of us into the kitchen to eat our sandwiches. Titania's cheeks were streaked with tears. The moment she saw Uncle Tristram coming through the door, she fled upstairs. I thought of going after her to tell her I was sorry about her pumpkin. But then I thought that, once she'd stopped weeping her heart out about that, I'd have to tell her that she'd probably been wasting her time decorating my leotard. If she began sobbing again, I'd have to stay with her to be polite and, downstairs, someone else would almost certainly look round the kitchen table and, not seeing me, reckon my sandwich was now up for grabs.

And I was *hungry*. Our snacks were lined up in a row along the kitchen counter, each with a little paper flag that had our name on it. I picked up my sandwich. It was delicious – plain white bread with a boring cheese, and nothing fancy added on or stuck around, to spoil it.

Under the flag that said 'Tristram' there was a torn-off hunk of bread that looked as if it might have been lying on the floor behind the bread bin for a week or two. It actually looked *grubby*. Aunt Susan hadn't even buttered it, let alone sprinkled it with pine nuts toasted in walnut oil. I didn't see a thing on the plate that looked as if it might have been pastrami. Or Roquefort cheese. There was no avocado. Or basil. The bed of rocket Uncle Tristram had suggested had been scaled down to one sad, droopy leaf of lettuce that even my mother would have dropped in the recycling bin.

And that was that.

I watched him staring at it. Then he turned to his sister. 'Excuse me, Susan. Is this *it*?'

Aunt Susan offered him the coolest look. '*So* sorry,' she said, not even trying to pretend she meant it. 'I realize that your sandwich looks a little primitive. But what with having to spend all that time searching for another good knife . . .'

Uncle Tristram looked around. 'You managed everyone else's well enough!'

'Everyone else,' she told him acidly, 'is being helpful.'

He didn't push his luck. He just picked up the plate and went to lick his wounds beside the sink. I sidled over and I urged, 'Go on, then. *Tell* her.'

'Tell her what?'

'What we agreed. That I'm the latest victim of the Mountfield Family Curse, and can't do the trapeze act.'

'Why don't *you* tell her?'

'You promised me *you* would. You said you'd tell her that I'd sell the raffle tickets for her instead.'

He glanced towards Aunt Susan. Pointedly, she turned her head away.

He sighed. 'Not sure that this is quite the time . . .'

'Why not? She's furious with you already. What have you got to lose?'

'I'll do it later. When she's calmed down a bit.'

'You *promise*?'

'I already did,' he told me irritably, just as Mum swirled into the room, still in her fortune teller's skirt and blouse. She even wore the headscarf with the golden coins. Sensing the atmosphere, she turned to Dad to ask, 'Is someone in the dog house?'

He grinned. 'Not half.'

Mum nodded towards Uncle Tristram. 'Is it him?'

'Who else?' said Dad.

Mum sailed across and stood in front of us. Snatching up one of Aunt Susan's glass dessert bowls, she turned it upside down and peered into it as if it were a crystal ball. 'I can see into the future,' she told Uncle Tristram. 'Even as I watch, the mists begin to clear. And I can see that you will make the same idiotic mistakes that you have made so often in the past. And not just once, but over and over and over, till the name Tristram has become a byword for foolishness throughout the land.'

She stretched her hand out. 'That'll be five pounds.'

While Uncle Tristram thrust his hands more deeply in his pocket to protect his money, my dad complained, 'For heaven's sake! I could have told him that for nothing!'

'Couldn't we all?' snapped Aunt Susan. 'Yes, indeed! Couldn't we all?'

Being so very unpopular had clearly set Uncle Tristram thinking because, as everyone loaded their plates into the dishwasher and drifted out, he told me, 'I'm just slipping up to tell Titania I'm sorry.'

'I'll come as well.'

He gave me quite a frosty look. 'Why? Just to watch me grovel?'

'No. I'd like to pick up tips on how to do it properly, because I'm next in line.' Catching his blank look, I explained, 'After all, as soon as you've kept your promise to tell Aunt Susan I've been struck by the family curse, I'll have to tell Titania that I won't be wearing the leotard.'

'Oh, fair enough. No reason you can't tag along.' He thundered up the stairs and beat his fist on Titania's bedroom door. 'Open up, toots. This is your Uncle Tristram.'

There was a silence from inside the room.

'Titania?'

More silence.

'Oh, come on, sweetie-pots! Open this door! I need to talk to you.'

We heard Titania ask suspiciously from inside, 'Oh, yeth? And why?'

Uncle Tristram took a deep breath. 'I've an apology to make.'

The door was finally opened. Inside, Titania, with reddened eyes, stood waiting.

'Can I come in?' asked Uncle Tristram.

'No,' said Titania. 'Not until after you've apologithed.'

'Oh, all right.' Uncle Tristram stuck his hands into his pockets and squared his shoulders. 'Titania, I'm really, really sorry that you're so upset about your precious pumpkin.'

To my amazement, Titania gave him the same sort of withering look he might have got from Aunt Susan. 'That,' she said, 'wath a weathel'th apology.'

'A what?'

'A weasel's apology,' I put in, to be helpful.

She turned her withering glance on me. 'Jutht what I thaid.'

Uncle Tristram was still looking blank, so she expanded her complaint. 'It'th not a real apology at all. It ith the thort of apology a *weathel* would give – one where you're not really thorry at all and are jutht trying to pretend you are.'

'For heaven's sake! I've just said that I'm sorry!'

'You haven't. All you've thaid is that you're

thorry I'm *upthet*. You haven't thaid that you're thorry you did it.'

I'm going to be honest, I *admired* Titania for sticking up for herself. I hate weasel apologies too. And when Dad tries the things on Mum, he always gets in even deeper trouble.

But I could see that Uncle Tristram looked startled. Then he firmed up. 'It might be nothing but a weasel's apology, but I'm afraid it's all you're getting. Because that's the truth of it. I am sorry that you're so upset, but I'm not sorry I did it.' He grinned at her. 'Because it was fun. And it was brilliant by the time I'd finished it. That is a show-stopping pumpkin you have out there now.'

'It'th abtholutely horrible!'

'That's as may be,' said Uncle Tristram. 'But it's so good that—'

I watched him scour his brain for an example, and thought I'd help him out. 'So good that, if you put it in the raffle as a prize, you'd make a fortune.'

'You certainly would,' he agreed.

We watched Titania consider. 'All right,' she said at last. 'We'll call it quitth. But only if the pumpkin thtill belongth to me.'

You could tell Uncle Tristram didn't think she'd want his pumpkin any longer than it took to start to shrivel, well before Halloween, and he would get it back. 'Right! Fair enough!'

The two of them shook hands.

'Oh, by the way,' my uncle added, 'I'm not the only sinner at your door. Ralph here has something to confess to you as well.'

'Hang on!' I said. 'We had a deal! You were supposed to tell Aunt Susan first!'

'He was supposed to tell me *what*?'

We swung round to see Aunt Susan standing at the top of the stairs, holding a sandwich on a plate and looking in no better temper than when we'd left the kitchen earlier.

'Nothing!' said Uncle Tristram hastily. 'Nothing at all. Honestly!'

And, for the life of me, I couldn't blame him. We waited for Aunt Susan to put down the plate and dip in her pockets for thumbscrews, or send for a torturer's rack, to try to find out more. But she just shook her head as if she had been expecting no more sensible response from Uncle Tristram, and turned to me instead. 'Ralph, I've a job for you. No one has seen your great-granny since before lunch. Please take this sandwich that I've made for her and scout around till you find her.'

'All right,' I said, and waited while she curled her lip once more at my nice rabbit slippers before stalking off. Then I turned back to Titania. 'Uncle Tristram was right. I do have something to confess.' I was about to spit it out – that I would not be wearing the leotard that she was brightening up for me – when she stepped back.

I saw it! It was hanging over the back of a chair. It was *astonishing* – covered in moons and stars, and with a sort of Milky Way of tiny silver jewels winding across the middle. Beside it, over the chair arm, there hung a matching cloak of soft black velvet streaked with midnight blue.

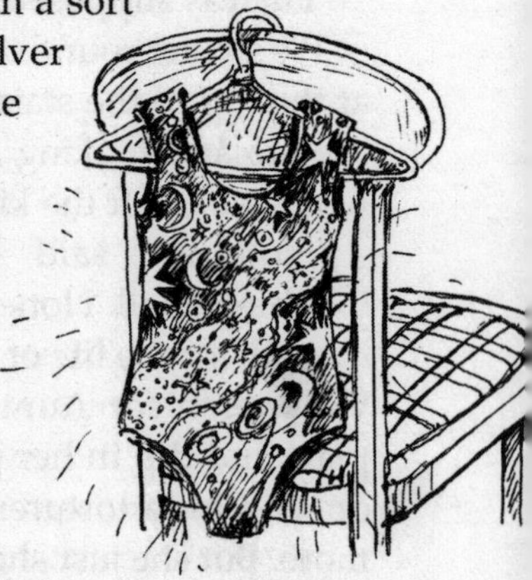

'That is *amazing*!' I burst out. 'I can't believe Mum's horrid dishcloth thing could end up looking like that! Titania, you're a real genius as a designer!'

She tipped her head to study her own handiwork. 'It ith good, ithn't it?'

'It isn't only good,' I said. (I was just being honest.) 'It is *brilliant*!'

'I'm glad you like it,' she said. 'What wath it that you wanted to confeth?'

Go on. Despise me. But I couldn't bring myself to say right there and then that there was no way in the world that I was going to wear it.

'Nothing,' I said, and looked to Uncle Tristram to help me out. But he was staring at the leotard in admiration and great wonder as well, and clearly couldn't bring himself to tell Titania the bad news himself.

BROKEN GLASS, SPRINKLED IN YAK FAT

I followed a trail of mashed bushes down to the lily pond, where Great-Granny was tormenting the goldfish with her sour reflection. I handed her the plate. 'Aunt Susan said this sandwich is for you.'

She peeled back the top slice of bread to peer suspiciously at what was underneath. 'What's in it?'

'Broken glass,' I muttered. 'Sprinkled in yak fat, and garnished with goujons of lard.'

'Don't mumble at me, Mr Potato Head!' she snapped. 'Speak up! Speak up!'

'It's ham and cheese,' I said a little louder, though you could tell simply from looking at it that it was roast beef with horseradish. (My very favourite.)

She was still studying it with deep mistrust. 'Oh, yes? Who made it?'

I took a chance and told her innocently, 'Uncle Tristram, I think.'

'Well,' she said, 'that one is Trouble in a Borrowed Suit. I wouldn't eat a sandwich made by him if I was a bag of starved cats.'

'All right, then. I'll have—'

Too late! She'd tossed it in the lily pond. Already the bread was falling apart in sodden clumps and goldfish were circling.

'That was a bit of a waste,' I scolded her. '*I* would have eaten that.'

She gave me one of her rattlesnake looks and turned back to the pond. I tried to gather up the courage to push her in. But though we'd done the history module on Superstitions only the term before, I still could not remember whether the body was supposed to sink or float, to make the peasants round the pond quite sure that the person they'd thrown in there was truly a witch.

SQUEEEEEEEEEEEEEEEEEEEEEEEEEK!

Back in the house, I found Dad in front of the mirror in the living room, practising his jokes for the show. 'So then the second police officer walked across the barn to kick the second old sack to check there was no robber in that one either.'

'Oh, goody!' I settled in a comfy chair. 'At last I'll get to hear the end!'

Ignoring my interruption, Dad pressed on. 'And so that robber, thinking just as fast as the first, pretended that he was a pig.'

'I'll do the pig noise,' I offered.

'Please don't,' said Dad. 'You won't be up on stage with me, so what's the point?'

'I *like* doing pig noises.'

'I've lost my thread now,' Dad complained.

I made a chicken noise while he was getting back on track. 'Be quiet!' he warned. Then, after a moment's thought, 'Right! So that robber called out, "Oink, *oink*! Oink, *oink*!"'

I couldn't help it. It is almost automatic: 'Oink, *oink!* Oink, oink, *oink, oink*, oink, *oink*!'

'Oh, do shut up, Ralph, or I'll throw you out.'

'All right,' I said. 'I'm going to sit here quiet as a mouse.'

'So then the third police officer decides, just to be absolutely certain there's no one hiding in the barn, that she'll kick the third old sack. So she lets fly with her boot and—'

'***Squeeeeeeeeeeeeeeek!***'

'Ralph!'

'That wasn't me!' I said indignantly. 'That was Mum's phone!'

It was too. Harry programmed in some ring tone called the Stamped-On-Mouse, and now Mum's stuck with it. No one but Harry knows how to get rid of it, and he's not telling.

It went again and sounded even closer. '***Squeeeeeeeeeeeeeeek!***'

We both went to the door.

Mum was outside, prising open her phone. 'Hello? Who . . . ? What . . . ? Where . . . ? Why . . . ? When . . . ? How . . . ?'

There was one last long pause before she said, 'All right,' and snapped the phone shut again.

'Well?' Dad demanded. 'Who? What? Where?

Why? And when? And last, but not least, *how*?'

'Tristram,' said Mum. 'He says that Digby's had a bad bump on the head. In that benighted tent. Tristram thinks he ought to go to hospital. To be checked out. Right now.'

Realizing she'd missed out the answer to the last of Dad's great list of questions, she added as an afterthought, 'By car.'

DOOMED TO UTTER FAILURE

'Well, there you go,' said Dad. 'Didn't I warn the world that letting Digby loose on a job like raising a tent was trouble in the making?' He set off purposefully along the hall. 'I'll tell your sister.'

Mum pulled him back. She looked quite horrified. 'We can't tell Susan! She's far too wound up to drive Digby anywhere! She would just crash into another car on the first bend.'

'In point of fact,' Dad argued, 'like everyone else on the road, she'll be a whole lot safer than usual because, instead of being at the wheel, Digby will be safely strapped into the passenger seat.'

'No!' Mum insisted. 'Susan can't go.'

Dad glanced at his watch. 'Well, Tristram can't take him because he's still in his cast. And you can't because Aunt Susan wants someone telling fortunes right from the moment they let the first punters in.'

I saw a way out of confessing to Titania about the leotard. 'I'll take him! We can catch a bus.'

They both ignored what I said. But Mum did give me that weird, narrow-eyed look she gets when she is plotting. Out of the pocket of her gypsy skirt she pulled a sheet of paper, and she and Dad inspected it.

'See?' Mum said. 'Ralph's trapeze act is not until almost the end of the interval. So he could take my place and do the fortune telling while everyone who doesn't want to hear the choirs is milling around outside spending their money on the stalls and hoopla and raffle and the lucky dip.'

'Me?'

Again, they both ignored me. 'I'm almost certain to be back in time. And if I'm not, he can just prop up a sign saying *Back in Five Minutes* and rush round the back and change into the leotard.'

Dad shook his head. 'That won't work,

Tansy. That gypsy costume is already swamping you. Ralph would look like a bedbug lost in a pillowcase.'

'Charming!' I muttered.

But Mum wasn't listening either to Dad's objections or to my complaints. Already she was tearing off the headscarf and unpinning herself round the waist. Letting the skirt fall in a swirly heap, she unrolled the jeans she'd folded up out of sight. 'I haven't time to argue. If even my irresponsible brother thinks Digby ought to see a doctor straight away, then I am taking him.' She unclipped the earrings, whipped the elephant-sized blouse off over her head and pulled her T-shirt straight. 'And I am going right now!'

'Tansy, you don't think it might be better if—'

Mum had snatched up the car keys. 'No! What does it matter if Ralph is rubbish as a fortune teller? He can't do anything special in a trapeze act, either. Just like you can't ride a unicycle. And there's no Mystery Celebrity Guest. And Harry walking around on plastic flowerpots is downright idiotic.'

She strode out of the door. 'I certainly hope the Toadpool Ladies have done a little better with all the stalls they've organized themselves. Because I reckon my sister's gone off her head with what she's taken on. No one in their right mind would let Great-Granny and her stick anywhere near a bran tub. And as for any raffle run by my brother . . .'

Words failed her, and she hurried towards the car.

Dad hurried after her. I hurried after him. Halfway across the lawn, Dad started up again. 'Well, how about if—'

'No!' Mum wouldn't even listen. 'This whole affair is doomed to utter failure! Susan should never have claimed that she could save the day! The only person in this house that I feel sorry for right now is poor little Titania!'

POOR LITTLE TITANIA

Poor little Titania?

I stopped short in my tracks. I didn't think I'd ever before heard the words 'poor little Titania' come out of anyone's mouth. 'That Great Big Fancy Show-Off' and 'Major Pain', yes. 'That Giant Cry Baby', when Harry and I have teased her once too often. Even, from Great-Granny's mouth (quite frequently), 'That little puff-ball with feet'.

But 'poor little Titania'?

Never!

Mum wrenched the car door open. Sliding into the driver's seat, she gave her parting shot. 'No one is going to say her father didn't see a doctor quickly enough because of us!'

And that was that. Slamming the door, she twisted the key in the lock. The engine roared. And Mum took off in a spurt of gravel to pick up Uncle Digby.

ACT THREE

ADDING A TOUCH OF STYLE

We stood there staring at the back of the car. Then I bent down to pick the bits of gravel that the car wheels had spat back at us out of my rabbit slippers.

Dad sighed. 'Well, that was quite a helping of Tongue Pie! But I suppose she's right. The most important thing is checking that there's nothing wrong with Uncle Digby's brain.'

Our eyes met. I was daring him to say it. And in the end he cracked. 'Well, nothing more than *usual*.'

We shared a chuckle, then Dad said, 'I suppose I'd better go and see exactly what it was that fell on Digby.'

'Oh, that'll be the tent pole,' I told him. 'It was leaning over anyway.'

We walked along the verge towards the

village hall. Outside there was a sign that said *Buy Tickets Here for the Prize Raffle and the Lucky Dip*, and on the table beside it Uncle Tristram was busy spreading seed-and-string vomit artistically round his pumpkin.

'I thought that table was put there in order to display the raffle prizes,' said my dad.

'It was,' Uncle Tristram agreed. 'I've moved the pumpkin here merely to add a touch of style to the tableau, and catch the eyes of any passers-by.'

'It certainly does that.'

We watched as Uncle Tristram arranged the various prizes that had been donated in semi-circles round his unhappy pumpkin. Since they were mostly ancient jars of home-made jam in drab and dingy colours, the whole effect looked rather good – as if these horrid foodstuffs were what had made the pumpkin throw up.

'Here,' Uncle Tristram said, handing me a leaking jar of something that called itself Carrot and Parsnip Chutney. 'There's no room left for this one, so you can have it.'

I thought back to Lady Leila's Stargazing Prediction that every Virgo would get a windfall, and Mum's prediction that it would be jam. I felt quite crestfallen until Dad snatched the jar out of my hand. 'You're not having that revolting mess! A pumpkin that looks as if it's hurling its innards round the place is bad enough. I'm not risking driving home with a boy doing the real thing.'

Putting his hand on my shoulder, he steered me firmly away from Uncle Tristram's raffle prizes, and towards the tent.

OH, DEAR ME. OH, DEAR ME

The tent lay in a crumpled heap.

'Well, there you go,' said Dad. 'Ask Digby what to do with your investments and you're in clover. Give him a practical job, and this sort of disaster is simply what you must expect.'

He stared at the tent pole and started humming some slow funeral dirge I took to be a tribute to the fallen.

I interrupted, 'Are you going to put it up again?'

He shook his head at the mess. Tent pegs were scattered all over. The ropes were horribly tangled. Canvas was billowing. 'What do you mean – "again"?'

'All right.' I corrected my question. 'Are you going to put it *up*?'

'I'm going to try.' He raised a flap of canvas. 'You'll notice Digby started with the whole tent inside out. That hasn't helped. Nor has the fact that he has stuck the wrong end of the pole into the ground.' He patted a couple of guy ropes, both of which instantly collapsed into pathetic loops. 'Oh, dear me. Oh, dear me.'

He set to work, pulling the loosened pegs out of the ground and turning swathes of canvas inside out. I settled down to watch, making the odd suggestion. 'Shouldn't that bit go there?'

'No.'

'Well, that flap looks as if it *should* go over there, behind that other bit.'

'Perhaps it does – to someone who knows nothing whatsoever about the art of raising tents.'

I pointed to one of the peg things. 'Aren't you forgetting to put that one in?'

'No,' Dad said shortly, and added after a moment, 'Ralph, don't you think that this would be an excellent time to go away and practise your trapeze act?'

'No,' I said. But the mere mention of the trapeze did set me thinking. In the end I just came out with it: 'You remember Mum said "poor little Titania"? Why does she feel so sorry for her?'

Dad twisted something round and clipped on something else. 'Well, wouldn't you? For years the child's been going to one class after another: to ballet, singing, dancing, poetry speaking, handicrafts. She's so keen to please, she passes every test they put in front of her, so the poor creature never stays in any class long enough to make a friend. And now, just because her pants got stuck to a lump of chewing gum on stage and one or two incredibly thoughtless members of the audience were mean enough to snigger, she can't so much as do a somersault in public without throwing up.'

The horrible knot of guilt growing inside me suddenly got worse. 'Perhaps that wasn't so much the sniggerers as the Mountfield Family Curse,' I said to him hopefully.

He stared. 'The *what*?'

'The Mountfield Family Curse. Fetched down on people by Great-Granny. It's like a sort of voodoo.'

'Where did that nonsense come from?'

'Well, Uncle Tristram,' I had to admit. And once I'd said it, it did sound like tosh. Dad certainly thought as much. He snorted with contempt, and went back to his pegs.

'Will she get better?' I dared ask after a while.

'I certainly hope so. It's probably just a

matter of her getting back her confidence.'

'How would that happen?'

Dad raised his head again. 'Don't ask me. People your age come from some parallel universe. Why, you could tie me in a reef knot and swing me round and round your head, and I'd still not be able to say what makes a single one of you tick.'

'Thanks,' I said. 'Very useful.'

'I find it safer just to stick to tents,' he said.

So, in the meantime, we just stuck to tents.

AN URGENT MESSAGE

After a short while, we heard whistling. A moment later, Uncle Tristram lurched up and lowered himself onto the grass at my side.

'Ah, Tristram. Come to watch the show?' Dad asked sarcastically.

'It's always useful,' Uncle Tristram said, 'to pick up tips. You never know when some poor weeping boy scout will need advice.' He leaned across and pointed. 'Shouldn't that bit go there?'

'No,' Dad said shortly.

'Well, that flap *looks* as if it should go over there, behind that other bit.'

I didn't miss my chance. 'Only to someone who knows nothing whatsoever about the art of raising tents,' I replied carelessly, as if I threw the things up all the time.

'Suit yourselves!' snapped Uncle Tristram, and sat there sulking for a minute or two. Then, just like me, he pointed to the peg thing. 'I think your dad's forgotten to put that one in.'

'Tristram,' said Dad, 'is there a reason for your presence here, or were you simply at a loose end?'

'Whoops!' Uncle Tristram said. 'Glad you reminded me! I have an urgent message. Susan wants you back.'

'Tell her I'm busy putting up the tent.'

'Can't. Then I'd have to tell her that it fell down. And mention Digby. Then she'd start wondering where he'd gone, and get in even more of a panic. So you go back to find out what she wants, and Ralph and I will finish putting up this tent.'

'Ho, ho,' my father said. 'Ho, ho, ho, ho.'

But he threw down the peg that he was holding and he walked away.

I waited till my dad was out of earshot. Then I said, 'Not sure that that was wise.'

But Uncle Tristram was in far too much of a snit to heed a warning. 'How dare your father "Ho, ho" me!'

'Nobody cares to be "ho, ho"ed,' I said. 'But now we have to put this tent up by ourselves.'

'He'd nearly finished.' Uncle Tristram scrambled to his feet. 'Look! All we have to do is shove this long bit here up through that gap, and fix these ring things to the end.'

I helped him push the canvas upwards. 'What, like this?'

'No! Not like that! Don't be ridiculous! How could it fit in there?'

'But this pole is supposed to go up there.'

'I don't think that can be right.'

'Well, your way isn't going to work.'

We struggled manfully for a minute or two. Then we gave up. 'I'm just not tall enough,' I said.

'What about Harry?' suggested Uncle Tristram. 'He's taller than you are, and he's just mucking about strolling around on flowerpots.'

'He's not just strolling around,' I told Uncle Tristram. 'He's learned how to twirl, and now he's practising jumps.'

'Really?' said Uncle Tristram. 'Jumps? On those tin-pot things?'

'They're not tin,' I corrected him. 'They're made of plastic.'

'Don't quibble,' Uncle Tristram said, and went back to fighting the tent. He shoved the pole this way and that for a while ('No, that won't work . . .') and then suggested, 'How about twisting this flap of canvas round like this, then trying to get that bit there over this loop?'

'I don't know,' I said doubtfully. 'I think doing it that way might have been Uncle Digby's big mistake. Dad said he had the whole thing inside out.'

'Nonsense!' With a great shove, my uncle got the tent halfway to upright. 'There! That'll do.'

'That isn't right,' I said. 'That's even worse than how it was before it all fell down.'

'Rubbish! It's safe as houses.'

'Only with you there, leaning hard against the pole.'

'You reckon? Watch me step away and prove you wrong!'

He moved away from the tent pole, which loomed towards us till a sudden breeze happened to catch the tent and flap it back the other way.

'See?' Uncle Tristram said. 'Pretty well rock solid!'

'Ho, ho,' I muttered. 'Ho, ho, ho.'

We had an elbowing race to get out of the tent before it fell. I didn't dare look back. But as we picked our way along the verge towards the house, my uncle turned.

'Still there!' he claimed with satisfaction. 'Nothing to worry about, I can assure you. Absolutely nothing. Nothing at all.'

BACKWARDS VOODOO

On the way back, I asked him, 'Uncle Tristram, do you believe that voodoo can work backwards?'

He stared at me. 'There you go again! Sounding all weird and feverish! What is the *matter* with you?'

I didn't really want to confess how guilty I felt. So all I said was, 'It's just that I've been thinking. Suppose it wasn't Great-Granny after all who put the curse on poor Titania. Suppose she simply lost her confidence after she fell on that chewing gum . . .'

'You think the Evil Sniggerers might be to blame?'

'They might be,' I admitted.

He shot me a shrewd look. 'And, if they were, would they be wondering how they might undo the damage?'

'They might be.'

He pondered for a moment, then made up his mind. 'Oh, I suppose it's the right thing to do. Admittedly, the way things are, we no longer have to sit and watch Titania leaping about doing her soppy fairy dances and endless tumbling displays, as well as having to listen to all her ghastly recitations and homespun songs. But it's a terrible shame for her. And she is so sweet-natured.'

I thought about it. He was right. Titania was sweet-natured. She must have spent weeks knitting all those soulful-looking Wumpies she hoped her mother would be able to sell for charity today.

'And generous,' he said.

That was true too. I hadn't even asked her to brighten up my leotard. She'd simply offered.

'And she's forgiving.'

'*Very* forgiving,' I reminded him.

'Yes,' he said. '*Very* forgiving.' And we both grinned, remembering the death threat painted on her bedroom wall, not to mention her slaughtered pet pumpkin.

'So,' I said. 'Any ideas on how to put things right?'

'What you suggested.' Uncle Tristram sounded confident enough. 'A bit of backwards voodoo. Since it was only loss of confidence that started all this off, I should have thought a bit of bolstering up Titania should do the trick.'

'How am I supposed to do that?'

'Listen,' said Uncle Tristram. 'I am your uncle, not the Toadpool Oracle. And I already have two jobs today. So sort it out for yourself.'

And he took off.

SWAP?

On my way back across the lawn I bumped into Harry, who was swinging Albert's flowerpots round and round by their strings so fast that they looked blurred.

'Swap?' he suggested.

I was so used to having the conversation the other way round that I came out with *his* line: 'Not likely!' Then I realized. 'Yes, please!' I said.

He held out the flowerpots and I was crazy enough to ask him, 'Are you sure?' before reaching out to snatch them. 'No going back!' I warned.

'Agreed,' he said. 'No going back.'

I clutched the flowerpots to my chest and felt as if a giant log had just rolled off me. I felt free again. 'You'll have to wear the leotard,' I warned my brother.

'Where is it?'

'In Titania's room. She's made it look quite special.'

'Really?' He looked suspicious. 'What? Glitter and pompoms and stuff?'

I wasn't going to let him change his mind. I shrugged. 'I'd say it was a sort of sorcerer's look. You know, dark cloak and moons and stars.'

'Fan-dabi-dozi!'

He took off at a run. And me? I was ecstatic! No more leotard! No more trapeze! And, as Mum said, anyone in the world can swan about on upturned flowerpots. Nobody needs to *practise.* I was so happy that I did what Harry had been doing when we met – I walked along swinging the pair of them round on their strings so fast they were too blurred to see.

BEEF AND HORSERADISH POISONING

Free! Free! I lay on my back on the front lawn and revelled in the feeling for a while. Then I got bored and looked up to see Great-Granny poking her stick into a clump of faded yellow plants with spotted leaves. I thought I heard a little squeal as something scurried away, and hatched a plan to pay her back for being mean to tiny animals – and throwing my favourite sort of sandwich into the pond.

I went back in the house. The gypsy clothes were still where Mum had dropped them on the floor. I gathered them together and, creeping up into Aunt Susan's bedroom, pulled on the skirt. Mum's safety pins were still attached, so it was easy enough to fix it round my waist. I transferred a handful of Dora's boiled sweets into the pocket, just to keep me going, then dropped the giant swirly blouse over my head.

Maybe I did look like a bedbug in a pillowcase, but once I'd tucked in some of the worst flaps and pinned the skirt tighter, I reckoned I might fool Great-Granny.

The earrings clipped on easily. I put the headscarf on, but I still looked like me.

I pulled it further down to cover more of my face. Now I still looked like me, but somewhat sinister.

This is a sort of show, I told myself. Like a performance. So what would Titania do?

The answer came at once. I went across to Aunt Susan's dressing table. I've watched Mum making up her face a million times, and it's not hard. I started with foundation. Then powder and eye shadow – I chose Gentle Lavender – with, finally, a rose-pink lipstick and some matching blusher.

Then I crept out and went back down the garden until I found Great-Granny. She'd moved on to scowling at another flowerbed.

I sidled up beside her. In a weird, flutey voice I said, 'Good morning, beauteous Lady. Cross my palm with silver?'

She gave me the sort of look that makes your socks catch fire. Hastily I skipped the begging-for-money bit, and went on to telling the fortune. 'I foresee terrible things ahead!'

Great-Granny couldn't have realized who I was because she was halfway to pleasant. 'Oh, so do I! That bank of alstroemeria plants for one. They're clearly dying. As for those rhododendrons over there, they are as good as done for with that blight.'

She waited for me to add some gloomy prophecy of my own, but I know nothing about plants, so I played safe. 'Those fish have had it, too.'

'Really?'

'Yes,' I said, and couldn't help adding bitterly, 'Beef and horseradish poisoning.'

'Good!' said Great-Granny. 'I have never cared for fish in tiny ponds.'

'Yes,' I said. 'All that swimming round and round in hopeless circles.'

'Depressing,' said Great-Granny. 'Not to mention gormless.'

'I think so too,' I said.

I'd never had a pleasant conversation with Great-Granny before. I was a little stumped. To fill the awkward silence that had fallen between us, I dug in my pocket and offered her one of my boiled sweets. Great-Granny waved it away. 'No, thanks. I've my own store of those fat, stripy ones.'

I turned up the flutey voice and stared out into space as if seeing visions. 'Would they, by any chance, be a gift from someone called *Dora*?'

Great-Granny stared. She couldn't bring herself to compliment me on my second sight. (I might have asked her yet again to cross my palm with silver.) But she did say, almost regretfully, 'I must move on, but it was very nice indeed to talk to you.'

'And it was nice to talk to you,' I said (a little shaken because it was true).

SEX AND VIOLENCE

I didn't dare go near Aunt Susan in the fortune-telling gear in case she asked me where my mother was. So I went in the tent and took it off. I would have stayed to rub off the make-up but the tent pole was swaying horribly and I got nervous, so I left it on. (Mum says good make-up is invisible.)

Then I went out to take a look around.

The Toadpool Ladies' Charity Guild had obviously been busy. Almost the whole of the village green was covered with stalls and entertainments: skittles, hoopla, ring-a-duck – even a popgun shooting gallery. There were refreshment stalls all round the edge, and signs to the portable loos. The Toadpool Bowling Club had mown a special patch of lawn to show off their skills. The Croquet Club had put in little hoops. I reckoned everyone from miles around must be involved and thanked my lucky stars all over again that I would not be in a leotard on the trapeze, failing to thread my legs through.

I walked back round to just outside the village hall. The bran tub had been filled. The pumpkin sat among the raffle prizes in its pool of vomit. A sign had suddenly appeared outside the wobbling tent:

and when I looked towards the steps I saw Aunt Susan putting up another:

Please take your seats for
the choir competition and the
interval show as soon as
the bell rings

To stay out of Aunt Susan's way, I slid behind the tent, to find Uncle Tristram busy setting out the tickets he was selling. He'd used up so much of the table top that Titania had moved her Wumpies onto a patch of grass.

Two had their weird long knitted arms draped round each other's shoulders. Another couple held hands. One baby Wumpy was in the middle of a somersault. A few sat in a semi-circle round a heap of tiny twigs and crumpled shiny red paper, as if chatting by a campfire. Two sets of twelve in differently striped jerseys sat on two tiny cardboard benches, looking like two separate football teams waiting to play. And one peeped winsomely round the cash-box at the passer-by.

'How many are there?' I asked.

'Forty!' she said with pride, placing a marble between one last small baby Wumpy's hands as if it were a ball. She stood back. 'Perfect! They look very thweet.' She turned to me. 'You're all made up already! I thuppothe I'd better go and fetch my pixthie outfit. Will you and Uncle Trithtram look after my Wumpieth for me?'

'Righty-ho.'

'I'll be back thoon.'

'All right.'

She'd hardly gone before my uncle ambled over. 'You're looking very weird. Perhaps you're feverish after all.'

'No, no,' I said. 'That's make-up.'

'Are you going to do a clown act as well?'

To stop him peering at me, I pointed to the grass. 'What do you think of Titania's knitted Wumpies?'

Uncle Tristram inspected the tableau critically. 'Is that the best she can do?'

'She said she thought that they look thweet.'

We shared a chuckle. Then he said, 'Sweet is one thing. Worth buying is another.'

'What's wrong with them?'

He cocked his head to one side. 'Too soppy, basically. I think we need a wider field of market attraction.'

'How do we get that?'

He looked at me as if I were an idiot. 'Same way as usual. Sex and violence.'

He set to with a will, rearranging the first pair of friendly Wumpies as if they were passionately kissing, and setting the other pair back to back, as if they'd had a major fight and now weren't even speaking. He turned the campfire chatterers into two loitering gangs and the two rival football teams into a furious mid-match mêlée, with carefully placed punches, and Wumpies throttling one another or pulling one another's hair. He set the baby Wumpy walking off towards the open fire without a babysitter. 'There! That's a little better.' He narrowed his eyes and frowned.

'I suppose, at a pinch, I could spare just a smidgeon of pumpkin vomit . . .'

'No, no! Titania will kill you!'

'She won't have time. We're starting very soon. Now what if I droop this Wumpy here over that Wumpy there, and make it look as if—'

I heard the gate creak. Turning, I saw Aunt Susan hurrying towards us. 'The choirs are arriving! The Toadpool Ladies need a bit of extra help with showing everyone where to go, so where is Digby? I have been looking for him everywhere.'

My uncle glanced at me uneasily. Mum had as good as ordered us not to let on about Digby's bump on the head. But no one in the world is brave enough to lie to Aunt Susan when she puts her hands on her hips and gives you the eye, so in the end, all he dared say was, 'Digby? Oh, don't you worry about him! He just went off with some woman.'

Aunt Susan was a bit put out to hear this, you could tell. 'Went off with some woman?' She gazed around in hopes of spotting him amongst the charity tables. 'But where?'

Nervously, Uncle Tristram said, 'To hospital, I think.'

'To *hospital*? Why?'

To anyone else, he would have told a giant whopper. But as it was, he only managed a weak stab at a half-truth. 'Because the woman suddenly got in a panic and thought they ought to go.'

Aunt Susan was exasperated. 'For heaven's sake! That's typical of Digby! There's a whole show to run, and he decides to drive some perfect stranger all the way to hospital because she's had some tiny little panic attack that would blow over if she just sat still and took a few deep breaths!'

It was quite obvious that Uncle Tristram found the next words very hard to utter. But it was a tricky moment, so he forced himself: 'That's Digby for you, Susan. I think you should be grateful that you married such a fine man with such a generous nature.'

I thought I'd better pitch in. 'I think you should be grateful too.'

It worked. Aunt Susan sighed. 'Well, if he's not around, we will need someone else.' She spun round to scour the village green. 'Where's Tansy?'

But by the time she turned back round to hear our answer, we'd both fled.

Dad strode up. 'Only five minutes till the Toadpool Ladies open the gates, so action stations!' He turned to me. 'You run and fetch Great-Granny. We need her by the bran tub.'

I raced back to the garden where I found Great-Granny picking a fight with a couple of uppity finches. 'You have to come along,' I told her. 'Uncle Tristram is selling the tickets, but Aunt Susan wants you by the tub to stop the children rooting about for ages in the bran, feeling for the best presents.'

Great-Granny looked at me as if I were a grease spot on a carpet, then went back to terrorizing the finches.

I raced back. 'She won't come.'

'Oh, Lord.' Dad glanced at the various choirs already being herded into the hall by the Toadpool Ladies. 'Listen, Ralph. No time to lose. So you go back and tell Natasha that there will be *vicars*.'

I didn't think I could have heard him right. 'Vicars? But *why*?'

He looked at me as if I were particularly dense. 'Because that'll make her keen to come.

Your great-grandmother has always greatly enjoyed quarrelling with vicars.'

'What about?'

'All sorts of things,' said Dad impatiently. 'Transubstantiation. The Efficacy of Prayer. The Problem of Evil. Justification by Faith.' He saw my blank face. 'For heaven's sake!' he said. 'Just everyday doctrinal matters.'

I didn't want to go unarmed. 'So what's Transubstantiation? And Efficacy? And – what was that other one you—?'

Before I'd even finished, Uncle Tristram interrupted. 'Don't even bother!' he warned my father. 'There's no point. Did you know that, till this morning, your son had never even heard of the Redistribution of Wealth?'

'It is a *mystery* what they learn in schools these days,' my father grumbled. 'Though I admit that Harry is quite handy at unscrambling the settings on all these handheld whatsits.' The two of them began to wander away. 'And, to be fair to Ralph, the boy can program that new digital thingy under the television when we go out.' He turned back briefly to flap his arms at me. 'Go on! Go back to Natasha. Tell her there will be *vicars*.'

Obediently, I ran back and bravely placed myself between Great-Granny and the cringing, shamefaced and apologetic finches. 'Dad says to tell you that there will be *vicars*.'

She gave me a suspicious look. Fearing she might start off at me about church matters, I just turned and fled. But when I reached the gate, I noticed she was coming after me. I led her back to Dad. He took her to the comfy seat he'd put beside the bran tub and told her, 'Just sit here and wait, and soon the vicars will come.'

Uncle Tristram was grinning as he moved off towards his trestle table. 'Sounds like some old religious prophecy: "Wait and watch. Soon the Holy Ones will appear".'

'Indeed,' my dad agreed. 'It does sound downright biblical. But wait till they get here and the scrapping starts. There won't be anything holy about that, I can assure you. It'll be like a catfight out of hell.'

ENTER PRINCE CHARMING

All this talk of prophecy reminded me of my own job. So I ran off to pin myself back in my swirly skirt and blouse, and clip on the earrings. I pulled on the headscarf again and looked around the tent. While I'd been gone,

Aunt Susan had set up a table draped with a black cloth embroidered with zodiac signs. And in the middle was a crystal ball I'd seen her using as a paperweight.

It looked good in the half-dark. I peered into it and, though my reflection looked like one of those distorted faces on the back of a spoon, I still thought I might get away with it so long as I disguised my voice.

Dad popped his head in. 'Ready? Because people are pouring in, and they'll be milling about for a good half an hour while each of the choirs checks out their placing on the stage, then settles in their seats. Make sure your customers cross your palm with silver before you start.' He pulled out his head, then popped it back again to warn me, 'And keep it *cheerful*. No getting bored, and prophesying floods and plagues of boils and the Black Death.' Again he pulled his head out then poked it back through. 'You two have made a pig's ear of this tent,' he said. 'I doubt if it will stay up long. That pole looks most unsteady. You keep your eye on it, and I myself will come back every now and again to check on it.'

'Righty-ho,' I said, not really fancying Uncle Digby's fate.

His head popped through again. 'And do

your Aunt Susan a favour. Be specially careful with anyone who looks as if she might be one of these Toadpool Ladies she's so keen to join.'

'Why?' I said, thinking with bitterness about the nature walks.

'Because,' he explained, as if to an idiot, 'if she joins them, she'll be a whole lot busier at weekends from now on down here in Toadpool.'

I grasped his point. 'Oh, right!'

Dad grinned. 'So that's your game plan. If anyone who might be one of her prey comes in, be sure to offer her the very best of fortunes.'

I told him fervently, 'I will.'

'Good luck, then.'

Dad vanished, and I sat there for a moment or two, practising telling fortunes under my breath. Then suddenly I heard a desperate scratching at the flap of the tent. In rushed the most handsome man I've ever seen. He looked like someone from a film, all crinkly cornflower-blue eyes and floppy blond hair. He spread his hands and flashed me the most charming smile. 'Thank heavens you're here! I need your help! Oh, be an angel! Help me!'

I wasn't quite sure what to do and so I warbled, 'This tent is fortune telling, not First Aid.'

'I only need to stay here for a minute or two. Till someone outside has gone past.'

I remembered Dad's strictures. 'You'll still have to cross my palm with silver.'

He scrabbled in a pocket, and offered me a generous handful of change. 'Is that enough?'

'I think so. Do you want a fortune anyway?'

He sat down. 'Not if you can't be bothered. I'm only in here to hide.' Again he shot me a most charming smile. 'You see, this gang's after me. Their leader is just going past.' He leaned in, lowering his voice. 'They're always trying to get me. Especially at this time of year. The end of summer, coming on to autumn.' He tossed his floppy hair and crinkled his bright blue eyes. 'Up until now, of course, I've always managed to escape. But sometimes, like today, it's been a very close-run thing.'

'Why do they want to kill you, anyway?'

'*Kill* me?' He roared with laughter. 'No, no. They want me to give them a lecture.'

'A lecture?'

'Well, half a lecture, half a sort of fashion show. About designer autumn wear.' He grinned. 'That's "woollies" to you. Expensive fancy woollies. You see, this gang's obsessed with making money for various charities, and that's the sort of thing they like: someone like me to come along and talk about my stuff, and sell it to the audience and give them a percentage for their good causes.'

I thought I might as well make my first visitor feel as if he'd had his money's worth from all that silver he had given me. So I leaned over Aunt Susan's round glass paperweight and fluted, 'Ah, yes! I see them in the crystal ball. They are all ladies and they call themselves . . .' I hesitated. 'Yes! Letters form in the mist. They are the Toadpool Ladies' Charity Guild!'

He reared back. 'I say! You are good at this!'

He rose and went to the tent flap to take a peek outside. 'I *think* she's gone. But she's quite cunning, this Mrs Blunt who's after me, so I'll give it one more minute, to be safe.' To fill the time, he gazed around. 'You are aware that your pole's on a shocking slant?'

'I am.'

'Oh, well,' he said. 'If anyone's going to know if this tent's going to collapse, it will be you.' He took another peek outside. 'I'm sure she's gone. I just wish that they'd pick on someone else. Why can't they find some lovely young fresh-faced designer who'd be thrilled to offer them a show? Why pick on *me*?' He tossed his floppy hair and flashed his charming smile. And we both knew why all the Toadpool Ladies wanted him.

Mum says that Harry could charm ducks off water when he tries. I do believe this man could possibly have charmed Great-Granny.

HARVEST ME NOW, LORD!

Next in was someone old, and crinkly in a different way. 'Are you the fortune teller?'

'I am,' I cooed. 'Come in and learn what is in store for you.'

'All right,' he said. 'Though I'm so ancient, I shouldn't think I'll get my money's worth.'

'Speaking of money . . .' I said, and waited while he crossed my palm with silver. He was the most wrinkled person I've ever seen. His palms were covered in brown spots, and his face looked like the contour map our scout master kept passing round on the field trip to Wales. But his white hair was combed in a neat parting. And he was wearing polished shoes. He might as well, I thought, have been my mum's first fortune-telling example.

I couldn't believe my luck.

I peered into the crystal ball and fluted, 'I see that you're the sort of chap who likes things orderly.'

'I certainly do.'

'And though you get on well enough with other people, sometimes their sheer untidiness and sloppiness can get on your nerves.'

'You've hit the nail on the head there!'

And I was on a roll. The words 'untidiness' and 'sloppiness' had made me think of my old teacher, Mrs Hetherington. I did a hasty brain search of all the other things that used to drive her mad.

'And you can't stand it when people spell things wrong simply because they're too idle to bother to look it up.'

'I can't! I can't!'

'And when they put apostrophes where they don't belong.'

He shuddered, making the whole tent quiver dangerously.

'And when they leave important things till the last minute.'

'It drives me mad!'

'And you're not crazy about scruffy hair or dirty fingernails.'

'I'm not! I'm not!'

We got on like a house on fire. I was quite sorry when I heard the next person in the queue tactfully coughing outside. I wrapped the session up with one quick prophecy. Mum had suggested I should keep it bland, like Lady Leila, and stick to windfalls and the like. But I thought that I knew what this fortune-telling customer would want most in the whole wide world. Our Mrs Hetherington was always clutching her hair and reeling around the classroom moaning that there was no hope she would live to see the day we'd finally learn the proper use of pronouns.

So: 'You will live long enough,' I prophesied, 'not to hear people saying the words, "Between you and I" when they mean, "Between you and me".'

He stared. You'd think I'd said he'd live to see goats camping on the moon. And then he looked ecstatic. '*Really*? I'll live *that long*? I must be fitter than I thought!

But that's a wonderful thought to take away. And when that Great Day comes – well, I shall simply spread my hands and say, "Harvest me now, Lord! I am happy to go!"'

Smiling seraphically, he picked up his hat and left the tent. Almost at once, his head poked back through the flap.

'I hope you don't think I'm speaking out of turn,' he said, 'but if I were you, I'd keep a very beady eye on that tent pole. The thing was swaying quite alarmingly all through our nice chat. I don't want to step on your toes. After all, you're the one who can see into the future. But I must say, the thing does not look safe to me.'

NOT A *REAL* PIXIE

I really hoped that my next customer might also be out of Mum's box of examples. But instead of a scruffy lady with toast crumbs down her front and tatty sneakers, in came a girl my age, wearing a stylish pair of jeans and a cowboy jacket. One of her tassels brushed against the tent flap. The pole wobbled horribly, and she took care to move her chair away from the direction it would fall.

'Come in, young lady,' I warbled. 'Cross my palm with silver.'

'It was my mum who sent me in here,' she announced. 'I don't believe in fortunes. In fact, I think they're rubbish.'

I warned her, 'You still have to pay.'

Rather unwillingly, she handed over the money her mum had clearly given her. I peered into the crystal ball. 'You're very smart,' I told her. 'Cleverer than most. And you're outspoken. So I expect, because of those two things, you sometimes find it difficult to make or keep a friend.'

Sarcastically, she said, 'Oh, *very* good!'

Remembering Uncle Tristram's way of being rude, I told her loftily, 'It is the sort of thing a chimpanzee could work out for itself.'

As if we'd reached some sort of insult stalemate, she suddenly stopped being horrible and pointed to the crystal ball.

'Please can I have a go?'

I pushed the paperweight towards her. 'Sure.'

She peered into its depths and grinned. 'I see the future and I prophesy that this tent will collapse around your ears.'

I peeped at her from under my headscarf. That strong sense of self-confidence reminded me of someone. And then my stomach clenched because I realized that that person was Titania – before Harry and I made a dent in my poor cousin's self-assurance with our horrid sniggering.

Is confidence catching? Can it brush off on you a second time from other people? Hoping my plan would work like backwards voodoo, I tugged the headscarf even further down over my face and warbled, 'And I see something in the crystal ball as well. I see you making good friends with a pixie.'

'A *pixie*?'

'Not a *real* pixie,' I corrected myself. 'Just someone dressed as one.'

She gave me the most scornful look, and bent over the crystal ball. 'I'm seeing something else as well,' she said. 'Someone who looks a lot like you being carried off, raving.'

I thought that it was probably time to end the session. 'And you will get a windfall,' I added, just to be generous. 'But only if you're nice all through the interval show, and don't do any sniggering.'

'Why should I snigger? After all, nobody in the interval show could possibly be any worse at what they do than you are.'

I made my only sure-fire, cast iron and un-arguable prophecy. 'Oh, yes, they can! Oh, yes, they can!'

KEEP YOUR HAIR ON, GRUMPY!

Dad came in next.

'You have to cross my palm with silver,' I warbled at him.

'Don't be so daft,' he said. 'I've come to check the tent pole.'

He shook it and it almost fell. 'Don't move!' he warned. 'Don't even breathe! Freeze till I'm back.'

I sat there, hardly daring even to blink. Then he came back with Uncle Tristram in tow. 'Sit on the floor!' he ordered him. 'Lean back against the pole to keep it steady. That's right. Now stick out your leg to anchor that loose rope with your cast. And hold this cord tight. Ready?'

I watched as Dad pulled tight some flapping strip of canvas and used the folds he'd gathered up to cover Tristram. Soon, only one arm and my uncle's cast were still sticking out.

'Right!' Dad said. 'Stay there, Tristram!

Don't even *think* of moving. Don't let it stray from your attention for a single second that I am holding you responsible for keeping my son's brain intact through the next half an hour. If you so much as sneeze, that tent pole's liable to fall.'

All Uncle Tristram said was, 'Keep your hair on, Grumpy!'

Dad left the tent. Before the next customer came in, I asked my uncle, 'Why's he so cross with you?'

The answer came out muffled. 'He thinks I did a shoddy job of finishing the tent.' I watched the heap of canvas shrug. 'And I suppose he cares about your brain – even though most of the conversations you and I have had today have led me to believe there's singularly little in it.'

Stung, I hit back. 'At least if I'd been given the job of selling raffle tickets, I would have managed to stay behind my trestle table long enough to do it!'

'Do it? I have already finished it!'

'You've sold them *all*?'

The canvas heap appeared to preen itself. 'I certainly did. They went like wildfire. The whole of Toadpool must be jam and chutney mad.'

I was still smarting from his rudeness about my empty brain. 'Well, what about the tickets for the lucky dip?'

'All sold as well. That spitting nun is much sought after around these parts.'

That disappointed me. I'd really hoped to have a stab at digging in the bran tub for that myself. 'Isn't there even one ticket left?'

'Not one.'

I told him sourly, 'You'd better shut up now. I'm going to get on with my fortune telling.'

'All right,' he said. 'And since I'm stuck here, I might try to have a little nap. If I should start to snore, just tell the punters that the rumbling they hear is merely the auditory sign of some benign psychic manifestation.'

'Is what?'

'The sound of some friendly ghost!' I heard him sigh. 'Honestly, Ralph, I don't know why your dad's so worried about the skull around your brain. It is the vacuum inside that worries me.'

I slid my foot out so that, if need be, I could kick Uncle Tristram really hard under the table.

Then, 'Next!' I called in my fortune teller's warble. 'Next!'

The next in was a woman. Leaning across the table, she shook my hand enthusiastically. 'Good afternoon! I'm Emily Blunt.' She wasn't at all the scruffy toast crumbs sort – more cardigan and sturdy shoes, like our head teacher. I didn't dare to order her to cross my palm with silver, but she did anyway. And then we started off.

Her fingernails were clean, but I could see some ingrained soil stained her fingertips, so, 'You are a gardening fiend,' I told her.

'I most certainly am.'

Her earrings looked expensive.

'Your garden's quite big too,' I guessed.

'Just a few acres,' she said. 'Perfectly manageable, so long as one doesn't fret too much about the tangles round the lake.'

I am not daft. 'And I see in my crystal ball that you have meetings with a group of ladies.'

'Yes, that'll be the Toadpool Guild. We're frightfully keen on raising money for the less fortunate. That's why I sent Esmeralda in earlier.' A tiny cloud shadowed her face. 'She told me you looked in your crystal ball and told her that she'd marry a pixie.'

'I didn't say that! What I said—'

I broke off. From beneath the table I could hear the sound of gentle snoring. I stuck my foot out and the noise broke off. By the time I'd dragged my attention back, Mrs Blunt had launched into a speech. 'There are always exactly twelve of us. We make a point of that. Twelve is the perfect number for a committee, don't you agree?'

Why should I argue? I've only ever been on the School Band Percussion Instruments Purchase Committee, and we were closed down by Mrs Hetherington for making more noise than the things we were discussing.

'Alas, though!' confided Esmeralda's mother. 'Moira has to leave us next month. She's off to northern wilds. It seems her mother-in-law fell down the castle well, trying to tame some disobedient creeper. So now it's Moira's turn to try to keep one stone set on another at the family haunt.'

I wasn't sure if she was on about castles or ghosts, so I just tossed my loopy golden earrings in sympathy and kept quiet.

'So now we'll need one more to make up twelve again. Someone who's good at organizing things.'

The snoring started up again. Again, I poked my uncle with my foot. The snoring stopped.

'In fact,' said Mrs Blunt, 'I have high hopes of Mrs Harlow, who has kindly stepped in to save the day by organizing an interval show during the choir judging.'

I was so keen to do myself a favour, I almost forgot to warble. 'Oh, Susan Harlow can organize all right! Why, she can even manage to get people who were perfectly happy sitting all by themselves, minding their own business, out on long, boring nature walks.'

'That's good. She sounds just right.' Suddenly Mrs Blunt looked just a little wistful. 'Though what would be perfect – absolutely perfect – was if, like Moira who is leaving us, she also had the one last thing we need . . .'

'What's that?' I asked, before I was distracted once again by sounds of snoring.

There was a most uneasy look on Esmeralda's mother's face. 'I can tell *you,*' she said, 'because you're a stranger. You're here today, and yet tomorrow you'll get in your little painted caravan and you'll move on. I wouldn't dream of sharing this with anyone else. But Moira was—'

Making a little embarrassed noise, she covered her face. 'Oh, I can barely say it! She was so *useful*.' Mrs Blunt took her hands down. 'There! Now I've said it fearlessly. She was so *useful*. You know – she knew half the world, and was related to the other half. *Frightfully* helpful when you're trying to organize things! Some of the others in the Guild are really hoping we'll find someone else like that. I have been telling them that all we need is someone who can *organize*. A smart and energetic woman! But they will keep insisting that she must also have—'

She broke off. 'What is that noise?'

'What noise?'

'That snoring noise.'

'Oh, that!' I couldn't quite remember what Uncle Tristram called it, so I said, 'That is a friendly ghost.'

'Nonsense!'

Before I could stop her, Esmeralda's mother had bent to look more closely at the heap of canvas covering most of Uncle Tristram. 'Who on earth is that?'

I didn't think I should let on that the untidy pile against the pole was Aunt Susan's brother. 'Oh, *him*,' I said. 'You mustn't mind him. He is just tired from putting up the tent.'

'Yes, but who *is* he?'

I realized she was worried that he might have

overheard. She wouldn't want what she had said getting about. And so, remembering what Aunt Susan had said earlier about the people who tend not to gossip, I tried to put her mind at rest. Crossing my fingers under the table, I said, 'Oh, him? He moves in different circles from you and me. He is a royal connection.'

She stared at me. And then she stared at him. '*Royal* connection?' She bent again, to peer more closely. 'Is that a *cast* on his leg?'

I thought she might be criticizing us for making someone with a broken leg help to put up a tent. 'It's nearly healed,' I said. 'He broke it weeks ago.'

'Really?' She leaned beneath the table one more time, but Uncle Tristram was quite hidden. All that was showing was a length of hospital cast.

Suddenly Esmeralda's mother shot me an

arch smile, and whispered, 'And could your mystery guest here under the table possibly have broken his leg while he was demonstrating a rather clever move in polo to a poor inner-city child?'

I wasn't going to tell her that Uncle Tristram did it when he was kicked out of bed. But on the other hand, I had to answer. So I just plucked at my swirly headscarf and warbled, 'I think you'll find that those, like the Harlows, who move in his circles tend to try not to gossip.'

'I knew it!' She looked as thrilled as if she'd won a television quiz with million-dollar prizes. 'What an amazing mystery guest Mrs Harlow seems to have found us! Oh, yes! The Ladies of the Guild will be *overjoyed* when I tell them.'

She rose. Halfway to the tent door she turned. 'It's been a lovely interlude. I've so enjoyed our chat. And may I just add that Esmeralda much admired your choice of footwear.'

I looked down and realized I was still in my rabbit slippers.

Mrs Blunt kept chatting away. 'I'm a plain dresser myself. We gardeners, you know! Happiest in our old wellies. But Esmeralda's quite the "*fashionista*", and she told me she thinks they add a charming touch to the whole gypsy ensemble.'

I suddenly had a brilliant idea for more backwards voodoo to help Titania. Looking down into Aunt Susan's paperweight, I called, 'Don't go! The mists are clearing yet again. And I see someone. He is tall and blond and handsome, with ice-blue twinkly eyes.'

She took a step towards me. 'Oh, I know him! In fact, I have been look—'

I interrupted her. 'He's very worried. Very worried indeed. He knows that while you're in the village hall you'll see the work of a quite marvellous, fresh-faced designer who would be perfect for your charity shows.' I laid it on thick. 'She's young – not nearly as young as she looks, of course. That "little cream puff on feet" look is just her current style. But she's amazing. Right now, she's specializing in leotards, but she can do anything. Anything! And so this crinkly blue-eyed man is hiding from you simply in the hope that you'll give up and leave before you see her stunning work on stage this afternoon.'

'Really?'

Again I crossed my fingers underneath the table. 'Really.'

'Well, then,' she said. 'I shall make very sure

indeed that I don't miss a single moment of Mrs Harlow's interval show.'

Just then the bell outside began to ring. Mrs Blunt rose to her feet. 'Oh, good!' she said. 'The choir competition is starting now. I'd better go and look for Esmeralda, so we can take our seats.'

'Goodbye!' I warbled.

Left to myself, I probably would have sat there for a little while, letting my Uncle Tristram's gentle snores calm my frayed nerves. But there were plenty of people in the queue outside who didn't want to listen to the choirs; and by the time I heard the bell that meant the interval show was just beginning, I had explained away an awful lot of snoring from the canvas heap, and prophesied at least a dozen windfalls.

FLOWERPOT MAN

While I was tearing off my swirly gear and pulling off the earrings, Uncle Tristram woke. 'Where are you going?'

'Backstage,' I told him, snatching up my plastic flowerpots. 'It's almost time for my turn on the stage.'

I saw him eyeing the massive skirt and

blouse I'd left in a heap at his feet. 'Don't even *think* of it,' I warned. 'During the time I'm being Flowerpot Man, you are supposed to be sitting right there and keeping up the tent.'

He grinned. But I'd no time to stay and argue with him. I just ran. I was quite desperate to get backstage in time to hear the end of Dad's first joke about the three policemen searching for robbers in the barn. But when I reached the hall's back door Aunt Susan stopped me. 'What's that on your face?'

I had forgotten she didn't know that I'd been telling fortunes instead of Mum. 'Make-up,' I had to admit.

'Oh, Ralph! You're all smeary! If you had wanted a little more of a stage presence, all you had to do was ask me.'

I could see Dad already on the stage, holding the unicycle. Straining my ears, I heard, 'And so the second police officer gave the second sack a really hard kick—'

'This way!'

Aunt Susan marched me off to the stage sink to clean me up a bit.

While she was wiping smears of lavender eye shadow off the tips of my ears, I asked her, 'Everything going well?'

'Swimmingly!' she responded. 'The hall is full to bursting and all six choirs sang well. The judges will be so hard-pressed to choose the winners.'

'Are the choirs out there, watching the interval show?' I asked her, suddenly a little nervous.

'No, no.' She took one last scrape with her cleansing tissue across my face, and then, mistaking my look of pain for one of confusion, explained, 'You see, Ralph, as a reminder that singing is at heart a friendly thing and not just a competition, the Toadpool Ladies give all the choirs one simple well-known song to practise separately during the interval. Then they crowd on stage to sing it all together at the end.' Her face clouded over. 'Mind you, I do think Moira Carrington could have taken just a little more care choosing the song. As far as I could tell, she just took one quick glance at the children's list of suggestions. She didn't even pull it out from under her purse to read the titles properly – just took a glimpse at the first couple of words and said, "Oh, that sounds nice and pastoral", and chose it.'

'What first couple of words?' I asked.

'Great green . . .'

A look of real distaste spread over her face. Her voice trailed off.

I shrugged. We'd sung a song in school called 'Great Green Killarney Mountains'. And there's a hymn we always sing at Harvest Festival that starts 'Great green fields that do yield our corn'. I couldn't see why my Aunt Susan might take against either of those. But there was no time to ask because she was already patting powder on my nose and pushing me towards the stairs.

'There! You look splendid! All ready?'

'Ready!'

I clutched my plastic flowerpots to my chest as I went up the steps towards the stage.

ACT FOUR

TWO THAD HEAPTH OF BONE

By the time I got up into the wings, Titania was on stage and Harry was standing waiting in his velvet cloak. (It did look *excellent*.) He gave me a quick thumbs-up, and then turned back so he wouldn't miss a single verse of Titania's recitation. It was one of his very favourites – the one about the faithful dog, Rocky, whose beloved master died of a heart attack up on the moors.

'*Colder and colder grew the corpthe*,' declaimed Titania.

'*Darker and darker the dayth.*
The baby rabbitth turned their headth
From Rocky'th thtarving gaze.'

I set down my flowerpots and peeped round

the edge of the curtain at the audience. Curiously, there seemed to be a good few more pairs of sad and soulful eyes gazing up at the stage than there were chairs. But then I realized that almost every child was clutching one of Titania's Wumpies.

'"Go back, Go back," warned Mrs Foxth
As thnow fell from above.
But Rocky could not leave the man
Who'd filled hith dayth with love.'

One or two younger members of the audience began to weep at this point. A surge of snuffling and the occasional *parp* of a blown nose accompanied the final tragic verse.

'Tho there the faithful pet did die.
And two thad heapth of bone
Prove to the world he never left
His Mathter all alone.'

Luckily for me, there was a positive storm of applause along with the wailing and tears. So while Titania bowed and smiled and nodded to the weeping audience, I got a couple of moments to try and balance my rabbit slippers on my flowerpots without the ears tangling beneath. It wasn't easy. The flowerpots seemed awfully wobbly. But I did reckon I had finally managed it by the time that Titania came off the stage.

Her mother was waiting for her. 'Enchanting, darling! Poignant and lovely! Now, quickly – into your pixie outfit for your next act.'

Aunt Susan turned to me. 'You're next.'

A HAIRLINE CRACK!

I hesitated. All I was doing was standing, yet Albert's flowerpots seemed to be swaying under me as if I were a ship at sea.

Thinking I was just nervous, Aunt Susan gave me a little push. I fell off onto the stage.

Turning my head, all I could see was row after row of large, astonished eyes. Hoping they were just Wumpies, I scrambled to my feet and tried again.

Balancing my rabbit slippers on the flower-pots, I grasped the strings. I had intended to start with something impressive – a few double jumps. But when I bent my knees, the flowerpot under my left foot seemed to cave in. I lost my balance and fell off again.

This time I couldn't face the staring eyes. But I distinctly heard a snigger. Getting up again, I set off more carefully, just trying to pick my way across the stage. Again, it felt like trying to walk on water as the flowerpots swayed and dipped and lurched.

And I fell off.

This time, there were more sniggers and they were quite loud. My rabbit ears got tangled in the strings. I had to sit and unwind those before I could get to my feet.

Then I fell over again. But this time, as I

reached for the first flowerpot, I saw the problem.

It had a hairline crack!

I reached for the other pot. The same again! Each of the flowerpots was split down the side. Harry had clearly done one fancy jump too many and then, instead of being honest and admitting he had ruined them, he'd passed them on to me to make an idiot of myself in front of the audience.

I looked into the wings. And there stood my brother, wearing his fancy leotard and grinning at me.

I couldn't help it. I just lurched across to grab him by the neck and pummel him into a pulp.

And I fell over. This time everybody laughed, even more loudly. I thrashed and flailed my way across the stage towards my brother, and every time I was tripped up by the splaying flowerpots or by my rabbit ears, the audience roared.

That's when I heard the whisper from behind the curtain. Aunt Susan's voice. 'Oh, brilliant clowning, Ralph! Well done! Superb!'

Clowning? You ask me how to spell it now, and I will tell you that clowning has six letters and one exclamation mark. R-E-S-C-U-E! For after that I had a really good time. I staggered round the stage, still making out that I was quite determined to walk on the flowerpots. It took no skill at all to look realistic each time I fell off. All I had to do was keep my face straight and appear to be still trying hard. And by the time I crawled off stage on hands and knees, trailing the ruined flowerpots behind me, the audience was back in tears – this time of laughter.

I'd been really *good*.

SO STYLISH! AND SO FRESH!

Harry was next. I waited till the lights went down, then slipped out and round into the audience. I didn't want my brother to know that I was keen to watch. The only empty chair was next to Esmeralda Blunt, so I took that. There was a drum roll, and my dad came on the stage carrying a long hook.

He reached up. Down swung the trapeze. My dad went off again.

There was another drum roll and Harry stepped out from the wings, flexing his muscles like a weightlifter. The audience gasped. I thought at first it was because of his muscles (though he doesn't have any) but then I realized it was the leotard that had astonished them.

It shone, it gleamed, it glistened and it sparkled. Under the bright stage lights it seemed to ripple with light. It was like watching stars in the Milky Way swim underwater. I took a sideways glance. Both Esmeralda and her mother were staring entranced, hands clasped. Mrs Blunt leaned towards her daughter, and I distinctly caught the words '*brilliant* young designer!' before she turned back to watch my brother bow and then, without a moment's hesitation, swing himself up backwards onto the trapeze.

And I admit that he was brilliant. For one thing, Harry is a show-off, like Titania. He will do anything to get a round of applause. And for another, he has no sense of danger. When he played the Cheshire Cat in our school play, he was supposed to sit very sensibly, cross-legged on a desk; but when the big day came he ended up on the top of the stacked chairs in front of the wall display (*Good Morning* written in forty different languages), all sprawled out sideways, showing his cool cat smile.

So, once he was up there, he did everything that you can do on a trapeze. He lay. He sat. He twirled it round. He shimmied up the sides.

He made the thing swing sideways. He made it swing so high that even I (who wanted him dead anyway) was worried that he might fall off.

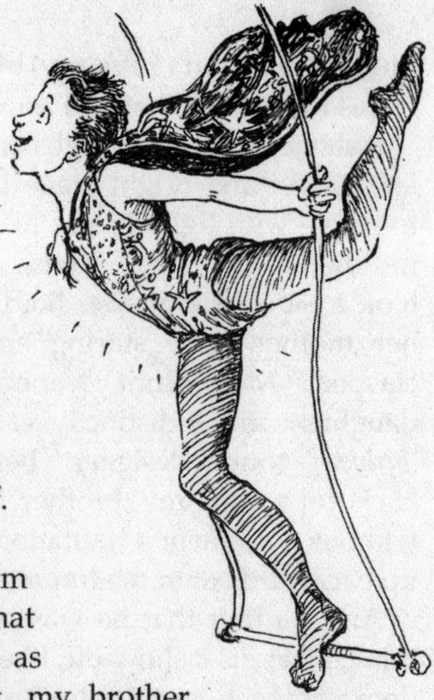

And even when the beam cracked with that sound as loud as any pistol shot, my brother didn't panic. As the ropes on the left-hand side of the trapeze slid off their snapped support, he simply made a star sign of his body and clung to the remaining rope. As soon as that, too, started its short slide, he deftly dropped down to the stage, collapsed in a neat heap and spread the hands he'd put up to protect himself as if it were one last stylish gymnastic shape to end his splendid show.

The audience roared. They thought he was brilliant. I saw Aunt Susan beaming in the wings, and as he finally went off after a million bows, and storms and storms of applause, she actually stepped out to kiss him.

Now Esmeralda and her mother were locked in excited conversation. 'Such *marvellous* sequin work! So stylish. And so fresh!'

'We *must* get the designer's name!'

'Whoever it is, he or she would be perfect for our next Guild fashion show.'

'And my school could order two dozen new leotards for the gymnastic team.'

'Moira could get an evening frock that shimmers like that for her Farewell Ball.'

This backwards voodoo stuff works really well. I leaned across. 'I know the person who made it.'

'Really? You know the designer?'

'I do,' I said. But knowing that the ghastly and embarrassing pixie song was coming up as soon as all the shattered bits of beam had been swept off the stage, I didn't feel like mentioning that she was my cousin. So I was a bit more round about. 'She's very close indeed to the lady who's organized this show.'

Esmeralda's mother's eyes widened. 'Really? Does she design a lot for Mrs Harlow?'

Thinking about the Wumpies, I didn't even have to cross my fingers. 'Oh, yes. She makes whole boxfuls of stuff for her.'

There was another drum roll, so Esmeralda's mother raised her voice, just to be heard. The problem was that all the people in the rows in front and behind heard what she said as well. 'Darling! I couldn't have come across a more suitable replacement for our dear Moira in the Guild. First, I find out that Mrs Harlow's mystery guest is actually Prince Edward! And now I find out that her friends include top-rank designers!'

THINK OF IT! HERE IN TOADPOOL!
ROYALTY!

The rumour ran around the hall like wildfire. 'Did you hear? Prince Edward is the mystery guest!'

'Is he in here? Is he watching?'

'Think of it! Here in Toadpool! Royalty!'

'Much better than Madonna.'

'Or Robbie Williams.'

'As for Bruce Forsyth . . .'

'Perhaps Prince Edward is in the seat behind. Go on. Peep round for me.'

'No, *you* peep round.'

'No, you.'

People were raising themselves in their seats to crane about. 'I wish they'd turn the hall lights up, so we could see.'

'It's just like being at a Royal Command Performance!'

'This makes the ticket price, which I had personally thought quite steep, seem very reasonable.'

'And *such* an excellent show.'

'That girl who pretends to be a child with a lisp! She is quite brilliant. What a wonderful spoof!'

'I've seen her often. I've no idea who she is, but her stage name's Titania. And she'll be coming on again soon, to sing her pixie song. I've heard that plenty of times as well, and it's an absolute *hoot*.'

'Look over there. Is *that* Prince Edward? There, in the shadows.'

'No, no. That's Albert Harples from the garage.'

'Oh, so it is.'

And so the whispering went on. And on. And on.

TELL ME!

I suddenly had a thought. I'd told Esmeralda something useful. She could return the favour.

'Were you here right from the start?'

She nodded.

'So you got to see the very first act?'

'The man with the unicycle? He didn't ride it, you know. He never even got on it. But his jokes were good. Everyone enjoyed them.' She pointed to the man in front of her. 'He nearly had a heart attack, laughing. And that woman over there practically fell off her chair when he came to the end of the one about the robbers.'

'Tell me!' I told her. (I was desperate.)

'What?'

'The end. The last line of the joke about the robbers.'

'Just the last line?'

'Yes. I already know three quarters of it. I just need to know the bit from where the third police officer has a go at kicking the third sack.'

She thought for a moment. Then, 'Oh, yes!' she said. 'So then the last police officer thought she'd better check on the last dirty old sack. So she drew back her boot and—'

'Shhh!' said her mother. 'There is a pixie coming on stage.'

Esmeralda dropped her voice to a whisper. '– and let fly really hard—'

'Shhhh!' scolded her mother again.

Esmeralda broke off, and turned her face back to the stage where Titania, dressed as a pixie, was getting ready for her song.

'Thith,' Titania was saying, 'ith a thweet little thong about a thad, lotht pixthie.'

I'd heard it last Christmas. And the Christmas before. I'll no doubt hear it next Christmas too. So I just waited till the music swelled, then I slid off my seat, ready to get back into my gypsy gear and tell a few more fortunes after the show was ended but before everyone left.

GREAT GREEN . . .

I couldn't get out of there. All the choirs were being herded back into the hall. I tried to force my way through, but clearly taking me for one more choir member being a bit of a nuisance, one of the Toadpool Ladies seized me firmly by the shoulders and pushed me along with the rest. '*This* way.'

Before I knew it I was standing quietly in a line, waiting for Titania's pixie song to end, then watching her bow again and again to quite tumultuous applause and limitless praise from the people in the seats beside me.

'By golly, what a skilled performance!'

'Side-splitting stuff!'

'So young. Yet such a *brilliant* mimic!'

With one last bow, Titania left the stage, and I was swept up the steps along with all the choirs. I stood, too crushed to move, between two choir boys in purple blazers as the bossy Toadpool Lady who had pushed me into line stepped forward.

'And now! Before the final song, here's the result we've all been waiting for through that quite wonderful, spectacular interval show. The winning choir this year is—'

She didn't leave one of those stupid long dramatic pauses you get on television. She just came out with it.

'Ford Manor School Choir!'

You could tell straight away that pupils of Ford Manor School do not wear purple blazers. Everyone around me scowled. A faint, embarrassed cheer rose from some other place on stage, and while the audience clapped – rather half-heartedly, I thought – a gangling girl in a blue jacket pushed forward to accept the trophy. Staring forlornly at her feet, she muttered something quite incomprehensible, then, wielding the trophy rather like an offensive weapon, she forced her way back to her own choir through the great crush on stage.

The Toadpool Lady turned back to the audience. 'And now! The very end of this quite wonderful show. The choirs' Great Communal Song.' She dropped her voice in a confidential fashion to share a memory with the audience. 'Only last year, the Marquis and I had the most restful weekend in a small castle tucked away beside the famous "Great Green Killarney

Mountains". And so, when I was given the list of possible songs for the choirs' last rousing shared performance on stage, it was an obvious choice to ask them to sing—'

Her eyes fell on the slip of paper in her hand. 'Oh!' she said, startled. 'It seems I didn't choose that at all.' A look of utter distaste shadowed her face.

Right! I thought confidently to myself. It will be 'Great Green Fields That Do Yield Our Corn'. And I can make a jolly good stab at standing here pretending to sing that.

But I was wrong.

'It seems,' the Toadpool Lady said, with scarcely veiled disgust, 'that the song chosen for the final performance is called—'

She took one last slow look, as though she couldn't really believe her eyes.

'Great Green Globs of Greasy, Grimy Gopher Guts . . .'

I don't think I have ever seen a body clatter off a stage so fast.

BATTLE OF THE CHOIRS

The choirs went at it in great voice. I like the song as well, so I pitched in.

'Great green globs of greasy, grimy gopher guts,
Mutilated monkey meat,
Dirty little baby feet,
Great green globs of greasy, grimy gopher guts
And I without my spoon!'

The trouble was, I realized, that some of the choirs knew a different version. Where everyone on my side of the stage seemed to be singing 'Dirty little baby feet' along with me, some people on the other side, and at the back, were warbling 'Chopped up baby parakeet'.

I liked their version better, so swapped over. So did some others. But the rest around me were really stubborn. And by the time we hit the chorus for the third time, I could tell from the strains on our nice straight line, and the odd elbow punch, that quite a bit of quiet scuffling and pushing was breaking out at the back.

Then I got shoved quite hard by some stubborn 'dirty-little-baby-feeter' standing behind me.

Crossly, I jammed my elbow back.

She pushed again. I turned round, ready to find her feet and stamp on one of them, only to see that a fight had broken out. A real big fight. I hadn't noticed up till then because every single choir member on the stage was so well trained that they kept singing. Perfectly. I even heard one of the girls' choirs soar into a descant.

'French-fried eyeballs boiled in blood,
Piggies' ears dragged through the mud.'

It was impressive. Rising to the occasion, I kept on singing too, even while I was shoving my tormentor's head under my arm and trying to pull it off. She kept on warbling as we swept tunefully along to the last chorus, every last one of us determined that our version of the words would prevail.

I reckon that it was a tie. Honour was satisfied, at least; and as the piano finished with one last flourish, all of us snapped back into our straight lines and took a bow.

The audience went wild. They cheered and stamped their feet. Some even called, 'Bravo! Bravo! Encore!' But I was bruised enough to be quite glad when three of the Toadpool Ladies came up to shoo us off the stage.

The one I'd realized must be Moira said, 'We have a few last people to thank before you all spill back into the sunlight and make the most

of the last hour of the Toadpool Show out on the green among the stalls and entertainments.'

I didn't need to wait to see Aunt Susan get her thank you and some flowers. So as the others clambered down the steps, and back in lines along the sides of the hall, I simply slipped away into the wings, and out of the stage door, back to the fortune-telling tent.

FINALE

HAVE YOU BEEN *DRIBBLING* ON IT?

Inside, I saw a gypsy reaching for my crystal ball.

'Hey!' I said. 'Don't you touch that!'

The gypsy turned. 'Ralph, I'm not peering into it in this disgusting state. It's *filthy*. Covered in grubby fingerprints. Have you been *dribbling* on it?'

'Mum!'

'Yes,' she said. 'Digby and I are back, so I thought I'd take over.'

I can't say I was sorry. 'So there was nothing wrong with Uncle Digby's brain?'

'Nothing at all.'

She tried. I watched her trying. Mum does her best not to be rude about relations in front of Harry and me. But in the end, like Dad, she always cracks. 'Well, what I mean by that, of course, is nothing more than *usual.*' She grinned. 'They even did tests.'

We had a good laugh about that. And then I said, 'Where's Uncle Tristram? Dad said that if he wasn't leaning against the pole to hold it steady, the tent wasn't safe.'

'Oh, that's all right,' said Mum. 'I sent him off because I found the missing master peg, and hammered it down outside. I think the tent's quite stable now.' She pulled the flowery headscarf straight. 'How is my queue outside?'

I took a peep. 'Already gathering.'

'Righty-ho. Send in the first. And, as you go, please mutter, "That was *brilliant*", so they all hear.'

I like to do my bit for charity. I went out shaking my head in absolute wonder. 'Quite astonishing! Amazing! I am *overwhelmed*.'

ARCHIBALD TOTTINGHAM

Further along, there was a crowd round the raffle table. Someone was loudly singing, 'Why Are We Waiting?' while other, less rude, people just hummed along or made a point of studying the time over and over on their watches and mobile phones.

Then I saw Uncle Tristram peg-legging it as fast as he could towards the waiting crowd. Sneaking up to his side, I put on my most innocent face and asked, 'Is the really important Redistribution of Wealth happening now?'

He looked at me with deep suspicion, then tossed his head. 'If any of the prizes had been worth having, naturally I would have made the effort to mark the ticket stubs and fiddle things so the downtrodden masses happened to win them.' I watched him stare out at the crowd of people fiddling with their up-to-the-minute slick-pads, wiping mud off their very expensive shoes and admiring one another's new waterproof jackets. 'But, as it is, who cares?'

'What is the matter?' I asked sarcastically. 'Was that Friedrich Engels bloke not quite so bothered about the Redistribution of Jam?'

Pretending he hadn't heard, my uncle turned to the crowd. 'Right! Pay attention! Time to pick the winning tickets.'

Everyone surged closer to the table.

'No need to panic,' Uncle Tristram scolded them. 'Plenty of jam and chutney for every winner. Why, there are even a couple of leaking pots of marmalade here at the back.'

'Jam? Chutney?' One or two of the people in the crowd exchanged confused glances. But they stood patiently as Uncle Tristram shoved the bucket full of folded ticket stubs under the nearest person's nose and waited till she'd pulled one out.

Uncle Tristram unfolded it slowly and read out: 'Number fifty-two!'

A groan of disappointment greeted him. And one triumphant voice. 'Me! Me! I won it! So it's *mine*!'

Reluctantly, the crowd parted and I saw Esmeralda making her way towards the raffle table. 'Ooh, goody! What great luck! But can I borrow a wheelbarrow to get it home?'

'You can't have *all* of it,' said Uncle Tristram sternly. 'Only one jar per winning ticket.'

'Jar?'

'Of jam. Or chutney, if you prefer. Or leaking marmalade.'

'No, it's the pumpkin I want.'

Uncle Tristram looked horrified. 'I'm sorry, but the pumpkin isn't in the raffle.'

'It's on the raffle table,' Esmeralda told him stubbornly.

Uncle Tristram was panicking now. 'No. That was just for show. To make you all look at the jams.'

'Excuse me,' said Esmeralda, 'but I have won that pumpkin fair and square. I bought a ticket. That pumpkin's on the table. I get to choose from what is on the table, and I have chosen the pumpkin.' She turned to the crowd. 'That's what we would *all* have chosen, isn't it?'

A host of voices shouted, 'Yes! That's what we would have chosen!'

'That is the only reason why we bought our tickets.'

'I was quite certain I was going to win it. I was reliably informed only this morning by Lady Leila in my newspaper that, as a Virgo, I was in line for a windfall.'

'And so was I.'

'Me, too.'

'I'm not a Virgo. But I had my fortune told less than an hour ago and was assured a windfall was coming my way.'

'I got that fortune too!'

'And me!'

'And I was absolutely sure my windfall would be this pumpkin.'

Exasperated, Uncle Tristram snapped, 'Pumpkins aren't windfalls. Pumpkins grow on the ground.' He clutched his head. 'Oh, this is *ridiculous*. I'll take a quick survey. Put up your hand if you bought your raffle ticket solely in hopes of winning my vomiting pumpkin.'

A host of hands waved in the air.

Uncle Tristram pretended that they were invisible. 'Now put your hand up if you bought a ticket hoping to win jam.'

One lonely hand drifted skyward. 'Me,' said a shy and modest little voice. 'I quite like jam.'

You could tell Uncle Tristram was put out at how his survey had gone. He warned the crowd, 'Well, you're all out of luck because this pumpkin's mine.'

A voice behind him said, 'No, it ith *not*!'

It was Titania, coming out of the hall still dressed as a pixie. Hurrying across, she stood in front of Uncle Tristram. 'We made a *deal*. And now that pumpkin'th *mine*. Tho if I want to let it be a raffle prithe, I can.'

'Quite right, Pixie!' shouted someone in the crowd. 'You tell him, Pixie!'

'Oh, all *right*!' Uncle Tristram turned to scowl at Esmeralda. 'Take the benighted pumpkin. Borrow the wheelbarrow. I'll just call out some other ticket numbers for the jam.'

'Don't bother,' someone muttered sourly. 'Nobody wants it.'

'Keep your old jam.'

But Uncle Tristram wasn't in the mood to take no for an answer. 'Oh, come on! Which of you is willing to take jam instead?'

Out of the pumpkin lovers, not a soul stirred. So Uncle Tristram turned to the man who had admitted that he quite liked jam. 'Since you're the only sensible person in our midst, you can have all the jam. What is your name?'

The man glanced around at everyone and smiled. 'I hardly think I need—'

'Come on!' said Uncle Tristram irritably. 'Your name, please!'

Blushing modestly, the man said softly, 'Well, as it happens, I am Archibald Tottingham.'

'Speak up!' said Uncle Tristram. 'I can't hear you properly.'

'Archibald Tottingham,' the man repeated. Again he looked around. 'And I'm so sorry I'm late. You see, I didn't pick up the invitation from Mrs Harlow until just after lunch. And then . . .'

But no one heard what he was saying after that because the crowd had started to drift away, all talking loudly about how astonishing it was that Susan Harlow's brother Tristram had turned out to be at least as bossy as she was – even bossier! And within moments poor old Archibald Tottingham was left talking only to himself, the local rock strata and all the jam.

It was a very sad moment.

WINDFALL!

I kept on walking around. I hadn't any money, and no one wanted to swap the things I wanted for a handful of boiled sweets. So I was getting really bored when I stepped between two stalls to see a gang of terrified children, all holding tickets for the lucky dip and pushing and shoving each other.

'You go.'

'No, you!'

'You first!'

'No. *You* first.'

'Scaredy boots!'

And who could blame them? Next to the bran tub Great-Granny sat in state. Her arms were folded tight, and she was glowering.

The children started up again. 'Dare you!'

'No. I dare *you*!'

I felt so sorry for them, so I asked a girl my age who had been hunching herself up over and over, trying to gather the nerve to make a dash for the bran tub, 'Why don't you ask your mum or dad to do the lucky dipping for you?'

She shrugged. 'I did. Twice. But they said that they couldn't spare the time because they were too busy looking for the Mystery Celebrity Guest.'

'For Albert Tottingham?'

'No. For Prince Edward. Everyone says that he was definitely around before the interval show. And there was a story going about that he'd be back again after.'

Now I felt doubly guilty. 'I would dare go,' I told her, 'just to show everyone that, so long as you're quick, you're safe. But I don't have a ticket.'

'You can have mine,' she said. 'I've just decided that there is no way I'm going anywhere near that scary old witch.'

I didn't want to tell her she was describing my great-grandmother. 'I'm sure she won't hit you with that stick.'

'I'm not going to give her the chance.'

Across the patch of grass, we heard her parents calling. 'Kerry! We're leaving now. We've heard Prince Edward was spotted peg-legging off towards the pub. We thought we'd go and see. So are you ready?'

'Here!' Kerry thrust the ticket in my hand. 'You take it. Otherwise it will be wasted.'

She ran off. I took a very deep breath and

turned to face Great-Granny.

But I was too late. A little girl had crept close to the bran tub and, taking care to stay on the safe side, had dipped her hand in the bran. She didn't have the nerve to fish about, searching for what she wanted. She just pulled out the first thing that her fingers touched.

It was a rubber monster.

Someone else crept up behind her. I heard Great-Granny growl, but still the second girl dared to stick her hand in the bran for just a second. She got a pencil sharpener. After that came a toddler. His elder brother lifted him up to reach in the tub. He fished about a little bit, and I was worried that Great-Granny would take a stab at him. But she just narrowed her eyes, and he ran off with a rather good clockwork chicken.

After that, almost everyone who had been waiting dared to take a turn. They dashed up, stuck in their hands, then rushed away, only stopping to take a look at what they'd won once they were out of reach. I heard a few sour mutterings along the lines of, 'That's *rubbish*, that is', and, 'This is for *toddlers*!' But nobody dared approach Great-Granny to complain.

In the end, I was the last one. I knew exactly which of the gifts inside the tub I wanted, and that it might take time to find. Great-Granny's eyes met mine and she inflated all her poison ducts. I knew that if I stood too near, or fished about down at the bottom, she'd bash me with her stick.

It wasn't worth it. So I turned away and, whistling, stuck my hands casually into my pockets to saunter off, pretending I didn't care.

My hand touched something hairy. It was the Christmas beard Titania let me have because she didn't need it any more to keep the dust off her Wumpies.

Great plan! Borrowing the jacket my dad had left lying across a chair, I walked behind Mum's tent to put it on and pull the beard on straight. Then I went back to the lucky dip. Waving the ticket at Great-Granny, I said in a gruff voice, 'My turn!'

Then I went lucky dipping. I dug and dug. I found the fancy new smartphone and the magnifying glass but, since I didn't want those, I pressed on, carefully feeling everything I touched till I was sure what it was. I think I even found the box of crocodile magnets (though I suppose they might have been animal soaps) and thrust them aside.

Deeper and deeper I dug, although Great-Granny was snarling really fiercely now, and raising her stick. If she had guessed that it was me, I know that stick would have fetched up on my bottom. But since she thought I was a strange old man with a long beard, she made an effort to control herself.

And then I finally found it: the nun that spits sparks as she waddles along! I could tell by the winder on the side, and the smooth wimple and habit.

I tugged and tugged, and out it came. So Mum was wrong when she said that there are no proper soothsayers. And Lady Leila was right. I am a Virgo and I'd had a proper windfall.

And it was not jam.

'You pushed your luck,' Great-Granny growled at me.

I thanked her in a strange-old-man voice. 'Much obliged, madam.' And then I startled her by racing out of reach. I tripped on some old rope as I ran off. A peg flew out of the ground and hit me on the knee. But there was no way I was going to stop till I reached safety. After that, it took a bit of time to blow the stray bran out of the clockwork winder. But when I tried it on the steps up to the village hall, the nun was *brilliant*.

Even in daylight you could see the sparks.

FROM MY LONG BLACK BEARD DOWN TO MY RABBIT SLIPPERS

Mum found me. As her shadow fell across my nun, the sparks flashed even brighter.

'Ready to go?'

'Already?'

'No point in staying,' she announced. 'Some idiot in a long black beard tripped on a guy rope and the tent fell down.'

Under the beard, I blushed. 'Sorry.'

She shrugged. 'I don't mind. But your father has decided that, far from being as unhandy as he makes out, your Uncle Digby has a plan to murder every one of us with sawn-through beams and falling tent poles. He thinks that Digby only went to hospital in order to create an alibi. And he would like us all to leave Great Toadpool straight away, before the Master Fiend's next plot is hatched, and we all die.'

I snatched up my spitting nun. 'I'm ready.'

Clearly the sight of me clutching a clockwork toy reminded her of Albert because she said, 'Have you remembered the plastic flower-pots?'

'They're ruined,' I admitted. 'He won't want them back.'

'More biting on the way.'

'Perhaps we could give him something else.'

'What have you got?'

I turned out my pockets. All I found was boiled sweets.

Mum pounced. 'Are those from Dora? I'll have one of those.'

I waited till her mouth was full before I asked her, 'Do you think they'll do?'

She shook her head at me. 'No,' she said, somewhat indistinctly. 'Toddlers can choke on boiled sweets. But we'll need something.' Slowly her eyes travelled down me, from my long black beard to my long-eared rabbit slippers. She pointed down. 'How about those?'

'My feet?'

'No, you great twerp. Your rabbit slippers. Albert will love them.'

'They're too big for him.'

'Well, he can shuffle around. And take them off to cuddle them. Or keep them until he's older and has bigger feet.'

'But these are *mine*!' I said. 'I want to keep them.'

'Fine by me. Just don't complain when you get bitten.'

'No, I won't,' I said. 'Because I shall be sending Harry round with the bad news.'

ALONG TO THE FROG AND NIGHTIE WITH TWO BEAUTIFUL GIRLS

Aunt Susan was waiting for us by the car. 'Guess! Guess the news! Just guess!'

'You've been invited to join the Toadpool Ladies' Charity Guild.'

'That, too!' Aunt Susan said. 'But this is even better.'

'But that's what you've been wanting all this time! What could be better than that?'

My dad said sourly, 'Digby's arrest for several attempted murders?'

Aunt Susan ignored him. 'Go on, everyone! Guess the best news of all. Guess who came to the greatest ever Toadpool Show and has been here all afternoon!'

'Archibald Tottingham?'

Aunt Susan swatted away the notion. 'No, no. I mean – yes, it is true that Archibald was here. But really, who cares?' She clasped her hands with the thrill. 'No, try again! Guess who was really, really here and has apparently just strolled along to the Frog and Nightie with two beautiful girls for a quick round of drinks!' She panted with excitement. 'And someone overheard him say he will be back!'

'Strolled?' I said cunningly. 'Strolled to the pub? Or sort of peg-legged?'

'Well,' said Aunt Susan, 'I don't think I would be breaching royal protocol if I admitted that the man I mean is in a leg cast.'

'What's royal protocol?' I asked my aunt.

She looked down her nose at me the way she always does when I don't know as much about things as Titania. 'Really, Ralph. It is time you started taking an interest in the world around you.'

Mum was quite irritated, you could tell. She herded Dad and Harry and me towards the car, and quite deliberately left Great-Granny where she was, shaking her stick ferociously at a trio of baffled vicars. 'I'm sure Digby's well enough to drive Natasha back.' She gave her sister a sweet smile. 'Or you could keep her overnight, of course. That would give everyone time to wrap up what is clearly turning out to be a very satisfying ecumenical discussion.'

Aunt Susan merely shuddered.

Mum turned to Titania, who was helping Esmeralda push the wheelbarrow in which the pumpkin sat in its own vomit. 'Goodbye, Titania. Sorry to miss your acts in the show.'

Esmeralda spoke up. 'But she was *wonderful*. A *star*! And she has promised my mother that she'll design the clothes for the next Toadpool Ladies' Charity Guild fashion show. And that she'll make lovely new leotards for the gym team at my school. And that she'll show me how to make my own special Wumpy. And that—'

'Well, now!' Mum interrupted. 'No more time to chat. We must be going.'

I took one last look back at Uncle Tristram's pumpkin. Titania, still in her pixie gear, stood right behind it, looking perfectly happy beside her new friend.

No. Not just perfectly happy. *Radiant*.

I took a chance. 'Quick!' I said, not even giving my cousin a moment to think. 'Turn me a cartwheel, Titania!'

She just can't help it. If there's a chance of showing off, Titania does it. So over she went. Perfectly, just as she always used to do before the snigger. Then Esmeralda joined in too, and soon the pair of them were wheeling round and round the garden, spending as much time upside down as the right way up. I think, if Uncle Tristram hadn't still been down the pub with his two beautiful girls, he would have been extremely impressed with the results of all my backwards voodoo.

I didn't say a word, but I felt proud. And almost cousinly.

Almost. Not quite.

POTATOES!

Without the handbag full of rocks and Great-Granny between us, it was a comfy ride home. As soon as we got in the house, Mum said, 'Thank God that's over. Who's for a cup of tea?'

Dad stared at her. 'After a day like that? *Tea?* Tansy, you have to be joking!' Turning to me, he ordered, 'Ralph, go find the whisky bottle.'

'Righty-ho,' I chirruped, and went to fetch it while Mum ordered Harry off next door to tell Albert the bad news. When Dad had blown the dust off the bottle and poured himself a drink, I begged to taste it. 'Certainly not,' said Dad. 'For one thing, it's from your Uncle Digby so it's probably poisonous. And for another, it takes the enamel off your teeth. So you just sit there quietly and drink your cocoa.'

I watched him sip and grimace and gradually calm down. And finally, when Dad had taken the taste of whisky away by chomping through more of my dwindling store of Dora's sweets, and Harry had come back, and Mum had stemmed the blood and put a plaster on his hand, I told Dad, 'Well, go on.'

Dad looked a little blank. 'Go on with what?'

'The joke.'

'What joke?'

'The one that you were in the middle of telling us this morning, when Aunt Susan rang.'

'That was *light years* ago,' he told me. 'When we were in a different world. That was before the horrors of the day.'

'Cracked beams.'

'Falling tent poles.'

'Blunted knives.'

'Psychotic grannies.'

'Vomiting pumpkins.'

'Ruined flowerpots.'

'And backwards voodoo for the family curse.' I saw them staring, so I stopped my own particular list. 'Nevertheless,' I persisted, 'I want to hear the end of the joke. The one about the robbers hiding in three sacks in a barn.'

'That's right,' said Mum. 'It's coming back to me now. One of them was pretending to be a chicken.'

Harry never misses his chance to do his

imitation of a hen. 'Cluck, *cluck*, cluck, cluck, *cluck*!'

'And when the second police officer kicked the second sack, the robber inside that one pretended that he was a pig,' remembered Mum.

'Oink, *oink*! Oink, oink, oink, *oink*!' I snorted.

'That's right,' said Dad. 'So then the police officers moved on to the third and last sack, and just to make absolutely sure there wasn't a robber inside, they kicked that one too.' He grinned. 'And, after a moment, from inside the sack they heard a rather desperate shout: "Potatoes!"'

I stared at him.

'That's it?' I asked. 'That is the joke? I've waited all day for *that*?'

Dad looked a bit put out. 'What's wrong with it? It's a joke, isn't it? It's *funny*.'

'No, it isn't,' I said. 'It isn't funny at all.'

It isn't often that Harry agrees with me, but he did this time. 'Ralph's right. No one in their right mind would laugh at that.'

'Everyone in the village hall laughed like a drain.'

'Well, they live in Great Toadpool and have to listen to Titania's recitations. Naturally they'd think a joke like that was good.'

Dad turned to Mum to referee. 'Tansy?'

Mum looked uneasy. 'Well,' she finally admitted, 'it is the sort of joke the boys used to bring back from nursery.'

Dad was outraged. 'I like that! You ungrateful pack! I have the worst day of my life, and then, though utterly exhausted, rise to the occasion on request to tell a joke, and all I get is rudeness and contempt.'

He pushed his empty glass away from him. 'That's it. I'm off to bed.'

As he was striding to the door, the phone began to ring.

'Don't think I'm getting that,' he said. 'Don't think I'm ever picking up that phone again. It's far too dangerous.'

He vanished through the door.

Mum slid off her counter stool and pulled her bag towards her. 'I think I'll go upstairs as well. I'm absolutely whacked myself.'

The phone kept ringing.

I turned to Harry as Mum disappeared. 'Do you want to get it?'

'No,' he said, hurrying after Mum.

I stood and stared at the telephone while it kept ringing. Once or twice before the answerphone kicked in, I even stretched out my hand. Then I thought better of it.

After the usual number of rings, there was a click.

I waited. And out it came, the message: 'Hello. Not back yet? Oh, well. This is Susan. I just—'

I didn't let myself hear any more. I fled.

THE JOKES

Dad's First Joke

After a bank raid, three robbers are on the run from the police. Hearing the sirens get closer, they abandon their getaway car and run off with their swag across a field.

On the far side, they see a barn, and rush inside to look for somewhere to hide. The only things in sight are three old grain sacks, so each of them snatches one up and jumps inside it.

In come three police officers. They look around but all they can see is three dirty old sacks. They're still suspicious so the first police officer kicks the first sack really hard. The robber inside thinks quickly, and then goes, 'Cluck, cluck!' pretending he's a chicken.

Then the next officer kicks the second sack. But the robber who's hiding in that one is just as quick-thinking as the first and, taking a cue from his mate, he hurriedly pretends that he's a pig, and goes 'Oink, oink!' as loudly as he can.

So the last police officer strolls over to the third and last sack, and just to be certain there's no one hiding in it, she kicks it very hard.

And the robber inside it isn't quite as bright as his mates. So he calls out:

'Potatoes!'

Dad's Second Joke

Three pieces of string are wandering about the streets, tired and thirsty. So one of them goes into a café to buy a drink. The waitress looks over the counter suspiciously and says, 'Sorry, you'll have to leave. We don't serve bits of string.'

So then the second bit of string decides to have a go. He spruces himself up and goes into the café and over to the counter.

'Hey!' says the waitress. 'I already told your friend. We don't serve bits of string in here.'

So out he goes, and all three sit forlornly in the gutter for a while. Then the third piece of string says, 'I have an idea!'

He goes out into the dusty street and beats himself up a bit until he looks a frightful mess, all scraggy, with pulled threads at either end. He loops a few bits of himself round a few other bits, and then goes off into the café.

The waitress looks at him suspiciously and says, 'Here, you're one of those bits of string that I've been sending away, aren't you?'

And the piece of string replies to her very firmly indeed: 'No! I'm a frayed knot!'

Dad's Third Joke

A man went to the pet shop to buy an unusual new pet. After a lot of thought, he settled on what the shopkeeper assured him was a talking centipede. He carried it home in a little white box, and left it to settle in.

Next day, he thought it might be nice to go to the park, so he said to the centipede in the box:

'Hey, do you fancy coming to the park with me?'

There was no answer, so he said, a little louder:

'Hey! How about coming to the park with me this morning? It might be really nice to meet a few people, and have a bit of fresh air, and all that.'

There was still no word from the little white box. So the man put his face down really close to it and bellowed through the lid:

'Hey! How about it? How about coming to the park?'

And then this tiny, tiny little voice came out:

'No need to shout! I'm putting on my shoes.'